REVENGE OF THE FLYING CARPET

Revenge

of the

Flying Carpet

J. M. EVANS

DERNIER PUBLISHING
London

Text copyright © J. M. Evans
Cover illustration copyright © Lorraine Cormier
This first paperback edition copyright © Dernier Publishing 2017

First published by Dernier Publishing as an ebook in 2016
Published by Dernier Publishing
P.O. Box 793, Orpington, BR6 1FA, England
www.dernierpublishing.com

ISBN 978-1-912457-00-7

Typeset by Pete Barnsley (CreativeHoot)

Revenge
of the
Flying Carpet

For my precious grandsons,
Issac and Toby

Contents

one

Flying Carpet

The one bad thing about flying off on a magic carpet was that I had to go with my twin sister. She got the celebrity name – Trinity. I got the boring name – Paul. And that just about sums up the whole of the fifteen years of our lives.

I never thought about revenge, though, until I found the carpet.

Trinity has always had the best of everything. She has thousands of friends – well OK, that's an exaggeration, but loads anyway, and she always gets everything she wants. If she asks and doesn't get it the first time, she wheedles it out of whoever another way, either sulking or making them feel guilty till they give in.

Mostly she helps herself without asking. If there's only one bag of crisps, she'll have it. She's supposed to be attractive (according to most people), gets A*s for everything, and is captain of the school netball team. So yeah, my sister.

I never stood a chance, really, being the second twin. Being the second everything. I'm just ordinary – plain brown hair, short and a "bit plump" as my gran is often telling me. I can't see much without my glasses and I'm useless at sport. I'm slightly dyslexic and drop balls. I just do. The only thing I'm good at is art, but hey, there you go. Life's not fair, as my dad used to tell me before he left us for a job in Australia. That was two years ago. He might come back, but he's got a girlfriend now, so he might not.

Anyway, I wanted to tell you about the flying carpet – well, it was the size of a large rug really, but magic rug doesn't sound quite right. It was both stunning from an art point of view, and for once in my life … hang on, I'm going too fast. Let me start by telling you how I found it.

It was in our gran's loft when we cleared out her house (she had to move into an old people's apartment with a lift because she can't manage the stairs any more). I had to pass all the stuff down the rickety loft ladder to Trinity, because it was dirty up there and I always got the worst jobs. A bare light bulb hardly lit up the cobwebs, let alone the stuff beneath. It was freezing up there (it was February), and the rafters were so low I kept bumping my head.

I nearly died when I first climbed up and saw how much dusty old junk was up there. You should have seen it, piled up high, stretching away to every corner.

My heart sank. What a way to spend a Saturday. We'd be here forever, I thought. I wondered where I was going to start, but it was obvious really – I had to start right there by the ladder because I couldn't get any further in.

I'll cut out telling you about all the tedious shifting and Trinity's non-stop moaning and whining, and get straight to the point.

The carpet was rolled up against the far brick wall, held up between a pile of chairs and a stack of boxes. I could see the blue wool on the edges, long before I could get to it – even then there was something about it. It was the only decent thing in the entire loft. Everything else was broken or rusty or mouldy or faded. I know this is going to sound strange, but the carpet seemed to be waiting there for me to find it. Even before I touched it, I felt kind of drawn towards it.

When I eventually did reach it, ages later, I unrolled the edge and stroked it. Tingles went up and down my spine. It was thick, warm and attractive in an arty kind of way, with a soft pile, like real wool, in shades of blue. Even then, I knew there was more to it than just the way it looked and felt. It was as if it wanted to tell me or show me something.

I was still feeling a bit *wow, I can't believe this*, when Trinity yelled up the loft ladder. "What's the matter slowmo?" Well I didn't want her to know about the carpet, so I quickly rolled it back up, slid it behind

3

some tins of old paint, and carried on shoving the stuff down to her, you know the sort of things – old lampshades, battered old suitcases, and a whole mass of decorating stuff that must have been our granddad's a very long time ago.

I waited for my moment. As soon as Trinity wandered off, moaning about her arms aching and needing a break, I unrolled the carpet and spread it out as best I could around the junk. Incredible it was, stunningly beautifully patterned, about the size of a double bed, looking perfect, not a bit dusty or moth eaten. And it wasn't as heavy as you'd expect, either, which was strange.

Then of course Trinity turned up, peering up through the loft hatch, leaning on the ladder. "What have you found?" she asked.

"Nothing," I said, but of course I had and she could see it.

"Liar," she snarled, pulling herself up the last bit of the ladder and into the loft. "Ooh, it's really disgusting up here," she added, wrinkling her nose. "Bit like you really." Then she turned to the carpet. "Hey, that must be worth a lot of money, I bet it's a genuine Persian rug. Nice one," she decided. "I could sell it."

"But it's not yours," I objected. If Gran didn't want it, I wanted it for myself. It's not like it was trendy or anything, I just really liked it.

4

"It's not yours either."

"I found it."

"Don't be childish," she said, looking down her nose at me. "I suppose you're going to say *finders keepers* next? Anyway, it's Gran's, and she'll give it to me if I ask her for it." As usual, I didn't answer. I just sighed, knowing she was right. Trinity, being deliberately annoying as usual, sat down on the carpet. She looked up at me in her superior way, with her arms folded, secure in the knowledge that she had won again, because she always did.

Well, as I couldn't get stuff down the ladder without her being there to hand it down to, I thought I might as well sit on the carpet once before it was taken away from me. So I stepped on to it and sat down.

Now this is going to be difficult to believe, but when I discussed it with Spencer afterwards (did I tell you he's my best mate?), we agreed that nothing is impossible. Well evidently, because with the sound of whooshing, the carpet lifted off the floor. I remember Trinity's horrified expression as we hovered for a minute over the ancient boards of the loft and the rest of Gran's stuff that we hadn't yet got downstairs, then somehow we must have slid through the roof because we were in the air outside and gliding through the clouds.

To be honest I don't remember much about that first journey, except that Trinity screamed a lot. When we landed a few minutes later, she looked a bit of a wreck. I have to admit, I was a bit breathless too. I mean, one minute you're in a dingy old loft in the freezing cold, the next you're in bright sunshine, on a rough path in the middle of a field of sheep in the countryside.

The sudden silence of not whooshing through the air was kind of really loud, and the hot stillness of the air was like being put in an oven.

Looking quickly round, I thought it looked vaguely Mediterranean, from the trees and bushes. The sheep were an unusual breed, so I wondered if it might be a rare animal breeds farm, until I saw three girls with stone water jars chatting at a well, a short distance from where we had landed. Yes, a proper well, with a wooden bucket and a turn-the-handle thing, and troughs for the sheep to drink from. The girls were looking at us curiously, then they started giggling, like girls do. I noticed, with a start, that they were wearing clothes straight out of a history book. Trinity went off towards them, still looking a bit shaken, moaning about magic trips, and why her, then stayed by the well, which was a relief.

I stood there for a few minutes, looking round at everything, probably with my mouth open. I felt completely out of place in my jeans and old grey hoodie, filthy from the stuff in the loft. All sorts of things were going round my mind, like, was this an interactive living museum sort of experience? Or maybe we'd stumbled on to a film set? My mind was reeling. Why had the carpet brought me and Trinity here, and what about going home?

I bent down to stroke the carpet and asked it, but there was no reply. Now I've written it, that does sound really stupid, but in my defence, it did feel like it had something to say to me. As I stood up, I got another shock. Two soldiers were striding over the hill, down towards me, in historical gear, complete with swords. I briefly wondered if I should run away, just in case they were for real, but it was too late; they'd seen me.

two

The Overcomers

They were for real, but I needn't have worried, both of the soldiers were really friendly. They raised their hands in welcome as they approached, as if I were an old mate or a long-lost cousin or something. Not knowing what else to do, I just waved back.

Cheerful they were! After the hello, beautiful place, lovely day type of thing, they asked me what tribe we were from (they must have thought I was with the girls at the well; maybe they thought I was the shepherd) and had we received our inheritance? I just jabbered some rubbish back, I'm not sure what, and they told me about their new place, somewhere a bit further to the west. Apparently it was by a lake with fish, with loads of good stuff around. To be honest I was just nodding and smiling. I didn't have a clue what was going on.

The younger man, whose name was Elishah, shared some water with me from his leather bottle and it was at last dawning on me that the flying carpet had brought us back in time as well as place.

It was so awesome! The soldiers didn't talk to me like I was a schoolboy, they talked to me as if I was a man – I guess in those days fifteen-year-old boys were considered adults.

It turns out they were surveying the land they had been conquering, so everyone got a fair share. Imagine that! They still had their weapons with them, in case the odd foe came upon them unawares.

Elishah, who probably wasn't that much older than me, showed me his sword – he was really proud of it and I was well impressed. It was unbelievably heavy and had jewels on the hilt. He showed me a few moves with it – you should have seen it glinting in the sunlight – awesome. He let me have a go, which made us all laugh. I was rubbish.

And his spear – talk about sharp, you should have seen the blade. I was glad I wasn't his enemy, he could have done some serious damage! Weird, isn't it, but it felt strangely like, if I hadn't had to leave, I think he and I could have been good mates.

After the talk about weapons, the older chap, Bildad (in his thirties maybe), said, "So how are you getting on in your new home, then? Better than walking in the desert, eh?"

Well that was a bit of a difficult question, since I'd

never moved house, and never been to a desert in my life. "It's totally amazing here," I managed eventually, with a bit of a gulp, looking round airily as if I knew it well.

Bildad sighed in appreciation. "Watered by God with rainfall from heaven. So much better than Egypt and the desert. We are fortunate to have had such a great leader as Moses, and a powerful God who has given us our Promised Land!"

And then it hit me like a football in the stomach. Have you studied Judaism in R.E.? Moses led the Israelites out of Egypt, then they wandered round the desert for 40 years before going into their Promised Land. *And I was there!* I think my mouth must have dropped open.

"Amazing, isn't it?" said Elishah with a grin, totally misunderstanding my overwhelmed expression.

"Yeah, totally," I agreed, trying to nod seriously, but with so much whirling round my head I could barely breathe. I must have gone back in time thousands of years, literally thousands! Why was I here? What was going on? Was it a trick or was it real? What could the carpet possibly want to show me?

"It's pretty hot; shall we sit in the shade for a bit?" suggested Bildad. "We're mapping the area." Sitting in the shade was a good idea – it was hot and I wanted a bit of time to think things through. I have to say, the sunshine made a nice change from London in February! I took off my hoodie, hoping the soldiers wouldn't comment on my Arsenal T-shirt, which looked a bit out of place, but fortunately they didn't seem to notice.

I think they were pleased to have a break from walking, and in the shade of a bushy thing they began reminiscing about their desert experience, which gave me time to get a grip on my slightly panicky thoughts. I sat down with them (after checking for sheep poo and stones), eager to listen, and I think they were glad to have someone to talk to.

I leant back on my elbows and closed my eyes. This had to be the most incredible thing ever! So magic carpets that flew ... real? OK so it was weird – still, this had to be better than sorting stuff in my gran's dusty loft.

I decided that if I pretended to be half-asleep, I could just listen, and maybe work out the reason the magic carpet had brought me here. Maybe it was just to give me a bit of light relief from my awful sister, I thought, as I lay there listening to Bildad and Elishah chatting and laughing.

Honestly, with my eyes closed, I could have been listening to a play set in historical times. They'd both been born in the desert. They talked with feeling about how cold it was at night and how hot it was during the day; how Elishah's mum was terrified of snakes after loads of people died after getting bitten; how some people never stopped moaning and how sand and insects got into everything.

Then they reminisced about the battles when they conquered the people who had lived here before them. According to Bildad they were given the commission by God to drive out the previous inhabitants, because they had become too evil for God to put up with them any more. Apparently the people who lived here before even burned their own children in fires as human sacrifices!

It was all so incredibly incredible, if you know what I mean. There I was, sitting on this hilly slope, in a field of sheep, talking to a couple of real life soldiers, thousands of years before I was born. After a while I sat up. They kept saying to me and to each other, "Do you remember when ..." which was a bit disconcerting, but as long as I nodded and smiled, they didn't seem to twig that I hadn't been there with them.

"God has given us victory over all our enemies," said Elishah at one point. His eyes had a far away look, as if remembering something special. And as I thought about what he'd said, my heart began to thump – that was it! God had given these people victory over all their enemies ... The carpet must have brought me here to show me how to get *victory over my enemy!*

As I was wondering what that might mean for me in practice (I was thinking I could ask their advice), the subject came back round to my home. It was their job, after all. "So where is it you're living now?" Bildad asked, getting a scroll out of his leather bag. "What's the name of your place?"

"Um, London," I stammered, my mind still half deciding how it was I was going to get victory over Trinity. They nodded blankly, like they had no idea what I was talking about.

"Not heard of that one. Which way is that from here?" asked Elishah, looking round.

"I'm not sure exactly," I admitted truthfully. "You can't see it from here."

"Don't worry," said Bildad. "If it's not on the list I'll add it." He unrolled the scroll and started running his finger down a list of names. I smiled with relief. This was going well! But then I saw Trinity striding towards us, and my heart sank. I'd almost forgotten she was there. She was bound to cause trouble. It was what she did.

"Come on, Stupid," she called in her annoyingly haughty way, as she approached. "Time to go home."

"That your wife?" asked Elishah. He sounded surprised by her rude manner. Or perhaps he didn't like being interrupted.

Trinity curled her lip at him in a very unpleasant way. "No, stupid, I'm his sister," she replied, turning her nose up at him. "And I'm here because we shouldn't be here and I want to go home."

"To London?" asked Bildad.

"Yes, it's much nicer than this boring place, but you wouldn't know it, it's foreign to you," she replied.

"Foreign?" asked Bildad with a frown, looking up from his scroll. She ignored him. A bad feeling was beginning to grow in my stomach.

Trinity turned her back on the soldiers and tossed her hair. She glared at me as if everything was my fault. "Come on, stop talking to these idiots and get back on the rug," she demanded. "I want to go home, I'm bored here."

I shifted uncomfortably and looked down. Under different circumstances I'd like to have stayed, but you know what Trinity's like, well you don't, but you're getting to know. She'd get her own way in the end whatever I did, so I might just as well go quietly.

At that moment Elishah noticed the carpet and strode over to inspect it. I trailed a bit behind. "Where does this come from?" he demanded fiercely, staring at me in a much less friendly way than before. "This is a foreign item."

"That's what I just told you," muttered Trinity, rolling her eyes.

"You're a spy," Elishah accused me, looking suddenly suspicious. "You are one of our enemies!"

"No, no, I'm not a spy," I assured him. I could feel myself blushing to the roots.

Trinity tapped her foot in annoyance at the delay. "He's a spy," she agreed. "The rug is for him to pray to foreign gods on."

Elishah and Bildad drew their swords. They no longer looked friendly. I could happily have sunk into the ground and been swallowed up.

"GET ON THE RUG," Trinity spat at me through gritted teeth. I didn't have a choice. I got on the carpet, which sailed into the air as soon as we were both on it.

I watched the soldiers disappear into the distance, until they looked like dots on the hillside. I didn't speak to Trinity on the way home (we did go home). I don't know why she wanted to leave. The girls were probably too nice for her. Pity. I would have loved to have stayed a bit longer. I could have signed up for Elishah and Bildad's army and learnt how to use a sword. They were the most interesting people I had ever met, and Trinity had ruined it, like she ruined everything. And the worst thing was, I hadn't found out how to get victory over my enemy.

But that was only the first journey.

three

The King

Spencer agreed that it was totally preposterous that Trinity and I had flown on a magic carpet. And it seemed even more ridiculous when he and I sat on it and it did absolutely nothing at all. It just laid there, like a ... well, like a carpet.

He did agree that it was an interesting design, but he didn't seem to feel the same way I did about it. Which was what exactly? Well, there was something indescribable about it. An extra dimension. Think what you like, I still felt as if it wanted to show me something. Something important. I tried to think what I'd learnt from the first trip about victory over my enemies (enemy), but the only thing I could come up with was cutting her up with a sword, which was hardly possible without getting into a lot of trouble (even if I had a sword). I thought there must be a principle I could follow, though.

Spencer agreed about that. He wanted to give the carpet a try, which is how we knew it didn't work for us.

We had to take it out of Trinity's bedroom when she was down the town with her mates the next day (Sunday) because she had, of course, claimed it as her own.

I haven't really described the carpet properly, have I? It had a kind of startling but gentle feel. The patterns around the outside drew your eyes in. Some of them were almost like a mosaic. In the centre, swirls and lines merged with images that seemed almost like pictures, but you couldn't quite work out what they were. It was an amazing piece of art. But Spencer's not really into art, so I don't think he really appreciated the beauty of the workmanship, and I'm not sure he didn't think I was going totally insane at first.

Anyway, whatever it was the carpet wanted to show me, it seemed it wasn't planning on showing Spencer. So with me feeling a bit small and Spencer being kind of polite, he listened to me telling him about the soldiers and their weapons. We played on the computer for a bit, then after he went home I tried sitting on the carpet on my own, but it still didn't go anywhere.

Then of course You Know Who came home from shopping and stormed into my room when she saw the carpet was missing from where she'd stuffed it. As if she cared – I mean, she had just shoved it under her bed. She probably only wanted to keep it because she knew I liked it.

I fixed my butt firmly to it when she came in. But

she was all mouth as usual and yelled and screeched and then tried to grab it from under me, and off we flew. Yup, you've guessed it, the carpet only ever flew when we were both on it. Sigh.

As Trinity was only grabbing the carpet, not properly sitting on it, she nearly fell off when it took off (which was what gave Spencer the idea to kick her off a bit later on). I have to admit that I didn't help her up as she scrabbled to get on. She wouldn't have wanted me to help, but I did make the mistake of smiling as she heaved herself up and made it to a sitting position. She assumed I was enjoying her moment of desperation, so of course, I was in for it straight away.

Why do some people have to constantly yell and scream and cry and make you feel guilty, even if you haven't done anything? I mean, it was her stupid fault she had grabbed the carpet in that annoying way. If she'd sat on it properly, like any normal human being … But as usual, I just let her get on with blaming me for everything, as I had done since we were born.

She didn't stop ranting and raving until we got to the King's palace. So now you know why I said at the beginning that the thing I hated about the flying carpet was going with Trinity.

Anyway, we arrived in the courtyard of this massive stone palace, Trinity moaning and shouting, and there was me, weary from the nagging, needing to get away.

That was another awful thing about being with Trinity on the carpet – you couldn't just get off or lock yourself in the bathroom or go for a walk – you're stuck on it. She used that to her advantage, once it had dawned on her that I was a sitting target, literally. Thank goodness none of the journeys took long.

But I was telling you about the palace. Well, I never actually went right in, although Trinity did. I don't know what era it was exactly. The King we met looked like quite young, as if he should have been at college. Cut a really kingly figure, though, he did, with long flowing dark hair and robes – like out of a film set. Anyway, as I was saying, we landed in the courtyard of his palace. It was impressive; you should have seen the massive stones and the carvings.

Nobody seemed to notice us appearing, but there we were. We got off the carpet and stood there, Trinity still stomping and stamping and spouting off. Four heavy-set guards in uniform must have heard her, and strode over to ask our business. Trinity said immediately, "I demand to be taken to the Queen," in that sarcastic way she has that makes most of her friends giggle, but there was no giggling here; two of the guards just ushered her away as fast as they could.

I wasn't arguing, it was a relief to see her go. Peace and quiet, nice one! So anyway, the two remaining guards repeated their question about our business.

They weren't exactly unfriendly, but I was umming and aahing, and wondering if I ought to pretend to be a salesman, or just tell the truth (remember, I hadn't got a clue where or when I was), when the King turned up with a whole entourage of people, including two servants waving massive peacock feather fans for him (it was quite hot again).

"*Make way for the King*," someone was calling. They weren't walking my way to start with, but the King stopped when he saw me. Some of his bodyguard people raised their spears, which was awesome, but he came over and asked me how I was. He must have thought I was somebody else, maybe a relative or an ambassador or something; I never did find out. But that's the thing about the carpet, there's something special about it.

I should have been frightened out of my wits, talking to a King, but it honestly felt like I was meeting an old friend. He said straight away how good it was to see me, then asked for news from the south, which was kind of handy since I live in the south of London. I racked my brain for the latest news. I was just about to tell him that a local government official was in trouble for getting a speeding ticket and lying about it, when I realised that wouldn't do! (I'd figured out by then, by the costumes, that we had gone back in time again.)

Then I remembered that a six-year-old girl had been abducted recently, so I told him about that. The whole of the neighbourhood had turned out to help look for her but it turned out she was already dead, killed by her uncle who had pretended to help with the search. I told him everything I could remember. He sighed. It seems that some things never change. Human nature, I mean.

Farmers had been complaining about the price they were getting for vegetables, so I added that too. He nodded again, then he asked about "the blessing of rain". I guess as it was hot there, there might have been a drought problem. Well it had been raining in the night, so I said so and he seemed really pleased and asked if the rivers were still low, so I assured him that there wasn't a problem, which was true. The River Cray was running normally; I saw it every day on the way to school, so I wasn't lying. Then he said, "That is truly a blessing from God." Most of the people I met on the carpet journeys seemed to think about God more than we do.

"It's a heavy responsibility, being King over God's people," the King continued, as he indicated for me to walk with him through an archway into a breathtakingly fabulous garden. God's people, I thought, that's interesting, and it all clicked into place … we were in the Promised Land again, some time after Elishah and Bildad!

The King stopped as a courtier ran up, bowed low, called him "my Lord" (which I mentally took down for future use), and they talked briefly about a problem with a vineyard.

"Yes, a heavy responsibility," the King continued, when the messenger had gone. "The lives of so many people depend on me. And in a way they depend on you too." I stopped in surprise. Since when had anybody's life depended on me? But of course, he thought I was someone else! So I carried on walking, and nodded, trying to look wise.

"Yes, my Lord," I agreed, copying the courtier, trying to keep it together. "I had never thought of my life like that, but it must be true if you say so." I was quite proud of that speech! The King nodded again and we walked along in companionable silence, the others walking at a respectful distance behind – there was a whole group of them, some scary-looking with weapons, in full livery. I'm guessing some were bodyguards. The others seemed to anticipate and fulfil the King's every need. Like one of them moved forward to take his cape when he was warm, and he'd only just moved his arm.

"Never forget, God is Almighty and cannot be mocked," the King continued. "Only if we do what's right will God save us from our enemies." I remember nodding sagely and muttering "exactly" every so often, while my mind was whirring. There it was again, God saving us from our enemies! Maybe this time ...

four

Authority

As we walked around the palace garden, and I was waiting to see how God might save me from my enemy, the King asked if I would honour him by joining him for dinner later. Well, what do you think? I wasn't going to turn that down!

I tell you, even just walking around this garden was like being in paradise. It was a bit like wandering round castle grounds on holiday, but more exotic. There were flowers and shrubs and trees, all shapes and sizes. Even the birds and insects sounded exotic, like being in a bird park. I've always loved gardens, even when I was little. I took it all in so I could paint it later.

While we walked, the King asked my advice (yes, mine, ha ha ha!). He had just been to the Temple, which the priests were supposed to be repairing, but money was short. Their country had had a few near-misses with wars with neighbouring countries recently, apparently, so a lot of spare cash had gone into their defence budget. I suggested they put a box near the entrance, with a slot in it, so everyone could put in their donation. I've been in a cathedral where they do that, I think it was at Canterbury. The King thought that was a good idea, so he talked to someone in his entourage and off they went to put the plan into action. Not bad eh! (I didn't mention the cathedral.)

Anyway we walked for about half an hour in the palace garden – it was the most amazing walk of my life, often in quietness, sometimes the King showed me a new flower or something, and told me what it was useful for – medicine and stuff. I didn't really understand much of that, so I just nodded and smiled. He talked to me about the different styles of architecture in the walls, though, and how the planting complemented the shapes, and how the soil affected what grew there. Now that was much more interesting, so I asked loads of questions and I think he was really pleased. He must have put a lot of thought into that garden. Probably his hobby, to take his mind off the king stuff.

You'd have loved it, too, even if you're not really into gardens. Anybody would love to just ride a bike round, or play laser shooting with a bunch of mates, or if they're not into that, just find a quiet corner to sit and read. There were sculptures, arches and pillars, walls and walkways, peacocks strutting about, hidden bits of garden with surprises in them, a row of orange and lemon trees with real fruit growing on them – it was totally awesome. At one point we stopped at a fish pond, where a fountain poured through the mouth of a lion. It was then that I decided I'd like to be a garden designer, like the ones on the telly. Imagine how amazing it would be to design gardens like that!

We were just watching the fish, enjoying the sound of the water running into the pool, the sun sparkling on the water, the warmth of the sun and the perfume of some exotic plants, when the peace was shattered by two more hefty-looking guards bringing a terrified prisoner towards us. They were followed by two more worried-looking men, making faces at each other as if in despair. The King stopped and frowned. I have to say, he wasn't a particularly smiley person, but this was a positive glower.

"Your Majesty, may you live forever," said one of the guards, bowing as best he could while holding his prisoner down. "This man was caught stealing money from a worshipper in the Temple."

I think I probably gasped. The prisoner moaned and struggled to get away, but with a guard either side of him he didn't stand a chance.

"Is this true?" asked the King in a commanding tone, rising to his full height.

"I beg you to have mercy, my Lord the King, may you live forever," stuttered the man, looking down at the ground.

"Answer my question!" demanded the King.

"My Lord the King, take pity on me, my family are hungry." The man was red in the face and looking scared half to death, although I have to be honest and say that he didn't look like he was short of cash. He was quite chubby and looked well dressed (for his day).

"I asked, did you commit this crime that you are being accused of?" demanded the King, almost spitting out the words. "Answer me!"

The man howled, which gave me a dreadful feeling in the pit of my stomach. The second guard spoke up. "We have witnesses, my Lord the King, may you live forever," he said, indicating the two frightened-looking men behind him.

"Witnesses, come forward," commanded the King, and after some more "may you live forever" stuff, they both admitted, with a lot of hand-wringing and cringing and bowing, that they had seen the man take money from the bag of a fellow worshipper.

I didn't know what to expect exactly, but I didn't expect to be present at a death sentence.

"As he has been proven guilty on the testimony of two witnesses, he must die," pronounced the King imperiously. "Take him away."

I think I was the most shocked person in the garden – everyone else seemed to expect the man to get the death sentence. The first guard put a bag over the man's head and led him away, while he howled and cried and begged for mercy. The witnesses followed at a distance, still wringing their hands and pulling at their beards and hair. It was a relief when they turned the corner and the cries faded away.

Then almost before we had time to breathe again, I heard You Know Who, yelling and screaming from one of the palace windows (we could see a corner of the palace from where we were standing). My heart sunk into my boots as the King asked in surprise, sounding annoyed at being disturbed again, "Now what is going on?"

My guess is that women didn't usually yell and scream in that palace. They probably don't in any palace, come to think of it. Can you imagine going to Buckingham Palace to visit the royal family and hearing yelling and screaming? Only Trinity could do that.

One of the servants who had been following us at a discreet distance dashed forward and bowed low. "I will go immediately and find out the reason for this imposition, my Lord the King, may you live for ever," he said, then sped towards the palace, holding his hat as he went. The King looked askance in a worried way in the direction of the yelling. The others were poker-faced. I'm guessing they were expecting another death sentence. I was the only one who knew what the disturbance would be; it would be Trinity, making a fuss about something because she wasn't getting her own way.

"I'm afraid that one of the women may have lost her mind," said the King confidentially to me.

Well, I couldn't speak. My heart was thumping. All I could think of was, would the King give Trinity the death sentence? Perhaps this would be final victory over my enemy!

"Would my Lord the King care to walk towards the hanging gardens, while we sort out the difficulty?" suggested another of his aides.

"No," he replied. "I wish to discover the reason for the commotion. Perhaps someone has died."

Well, of course nobody had died. (Apart from the man who had been sentenced to death I suppose.) Two more guards came out, leading Trinity, who was kicking and screaming, while they tried to avoid her kicks and blows. I just stood and watched with the others, as she was half-carried, half-dragged towards us.

"My Lord the King, may you live for ever, this woman says she's with the visitor," said one of the guards, looking at me, then grimaced in pain as Trinity bit his hand. "Aagh," he yelled, then apologised to the

King. "She was rude and insolent to the Queen, my Lord the King, may you live for ever." The other guard was holding Trinity in a stranglehold, with his hand over her mouth.

The King turned to me, looking both shocked and disgusted. "Is this woman with you?"

I sighed, deciding that honesty was the best policy. "Yes, she's with me. She's my sister." I was guessing that dinner was off.

"Does she always behave in this manner?" asked the King, his voice rising in anger. "This is completely unacceptable. Take her away, and do not ever bring her here again." He stalked off towards the palace, probably to check that his Queen was OK. The rest of his entourage followed, with barely a glance at me. No death sentence then. I sighed; it had been nice to have respect, even if only for an hour. Would Trinity always ruin everything good I ever did?

The guard asked me what I wanted him to do with the still screaming and struggling Pain in the Neck (he didn't call her that). I stood there, thinking for a moment. My heart gave a sudden leap – could this be my chance? I thought briefly about the King's matter of fact statement that I had the power of life and death, and was just about to open my mouth to tell the guard that she must die, when I closed it again. I opened and closed it again, twice, but I just couldn't do it.

So I told him loftily that tying her up was a good idea, and would he escort us back to the courtyard? He produced a rope and tied her hands behind her back, tight, while she screamed blue murder.

My first feeling was regret that I had chickened out. Then I remembered something important. The carpet wouldn't have flown with just me on it, and I was no longer in the King's good books, so how could I have stayed? And anyway, could I really have had her death on my conscience? Having the power of life and death is overestimated, I reckon. It's a lot scarier than you think.

The guard would probably have liked to have killed her himself, by the time he was done, but he walked us back to the courtyard in silence. Well, I walked, he dragged Trinity, still yelling, biting, kicking and screaming. He left us by the carpet, which we both stepped on to. I sat down as far away from Trinity as I could as it sailed off and away.

five

Ruined

Once again my time away had been ruined. I could have had dinner with a real king. I wondered what would have been on the menu. Perhaps a fancy roast type of meal – pheasant maybe, or a hog roast? Not chicken nuggets and oven chips, I thought disconsolately as I pushed the hard, tasteless shapes around my plate later that day.

"Is anything up, Paul?" asked my mum. Laurence was eating with us. Laurence is Mum's boyfriend. The last thing I wanted to do was to talk, especially with him there.

Trinity flounced in. "Sorry I'm so late for dinner Mum. I love you, but I was on Skype with Karlie, so I couldn't come straight away." Then she growled in my direction.

"It's OK love, I quite understand," said Mum then turned back to me. "You didn't answer me, Paul. You OK?"

"Yeah, I'm fine," I said, comparing in my mind the King's beautiful palace garden with our kitchen, and my civilised conversation with the King with the uncomfortable silence of Laurence being there. And now Trinity. Mum was OK when she was on her own, but when they were both there I didn't stand a chance.

"That hateful slime of a brother tied me up!" Trinity said loudly and loftily, slamming her dinner into the microwave. There was an astonished silence while the microwave whirred and Trinity stood there glaring at me, then an even bigger silence after it pinged.

I expect I sighed, like I usually did. Anyway, the upshot was, I tried to explain that it wasn't me, but it sounded pretty lame when Trinity showed the rope burns around her wrists, and insisted loudly and without stopping that it was all my fault. Well, I could hardly explain that it was a guard who had tied her up, could I? And that I had actually spared her life, and that the ropes had disappeared on the way back home on a magic carpet? They'd have had me locked up.

Then Mum started to get emotional when I observed (truthfully, I thought) that Trinity deserved to be tied up, and then Trinity went bawling over to Mum for a hug and sniffled in her shoulder, while giving me smirking looks behind her back. So I lost again, nothing new there.

Mum tearfully asked me to apologise, while muttering soothing things to Trinity. I did, through gritted teeth, and didn't bother with pudding. But as I was walking upstairs, I remembered that the carpet had taken me to two places where people had got victory over their enemies. There had to be something in that.

* * * * *

The way the next trip started was even more ridiculous than the first two. It was to an olive grove. I met a nice old man there, who seemed to know me better than I know myself. In a good way. It started in my room again, which is the smallest room in the house – even the bathroom is bigger. Trinity has the largest bedroom of course – she wheeled it out of Mum when Dad left, no surprises there.

Well, Trinity was being nice to me. I smelt a rat of course. So when she came in and asked if she could sit on the carpet, I agreed, slightly nervously. She didn't usually ask for stuff, she just took what she wanted. (She had left the carpet in my room in a huff after the last trip.)

I was sitting on my bed at the time, doing some sketches on the laptop for paintings I was planning on doing at some point. Images from where we'd been. I had two so far – the King standing by the lion fountain in his garden, surrounded by bushes with brightly coloured flowers, and an archway beyond, through which you could see a bit of the palace. The second one was Elishah showing me moves with his sword, with Bildad watching. I'd decided not to put myself in the pictures, because the clothing would be all wrong. And I certainly wasn't going to paint Trinity in. I saw enough of her in real life.

Anyway, we sat in silence for a while, then Trinity said, "That rug, it only works when we're both sitting on it."

"Yeah," I agreed, wishing she'd go.

"Have you tried it on your own?"

"Yeah." I didn't say I'd tried it with Spencer.

"So, you want to go on an adventure now?"

"No."

"Why not?"

I didn't look up. I didn't reply, either. She was starting to sound demanding, and that made me feel uncomfortable. Plus, I wanted to choose my words carefully. She needed wise handling if I was to survive, I'd learnt that from the cradle.

Trinity shifted on the carpet and tried to pick out some bits of wool. "So, why not?"

"Don't pull out the wool," I cried out in horror, forgetting the need for wise handling. So of course she tugged harder and a clump of blue strands came away in her hand. She grinned and waved them in my direction. I was furious. I've already told you, there was something about that carpet, and I was attached to it.

"I'll stop if you get on it," she said in her most annoying, whining voice, twisting another few strands round her fingers to get a better grip.

I lunged at her to make her stop. My bedroom's small; there's only room for my bed, a chest of drawers, and a cupboard at the bottom of the bed that does for wardrobe and everything else as well, so the carpet took up all the spare space on the floor. So as I lunged to stop her, I landed on the carpet ... and off we went.

six

Understanding

I was really mad this time – how dare she pull bits out of the carpet and force me on it! There was nothing I could do about it though – I was just glad that my laptop had not come with us. In my urgency to get Trinity to stop, I must have chucked it down on the bed. My work probably wouldn't be saved, I thought gloomily, but hey, that's life with the Worst Sister in the World. (If you tell me yours is worse I won't believe you; it's simply not possible to be worse than Trinity.)

So off we flew, fighting and arguing all the way about whether it was OK to pull bits off the carpet or not. Sigh.

We were still arguing when we arrived in this quiet grove of olive trees. Trinity had been holding the strands of wool out of my reach as I tried to grab them. Pathetic, isn't it? I managed to grab them out of her hand and put them in my pocket just as we landed. She immediately tried to grab them back as we both stood up. I was fending her off when I noticed an old man sitting on a wooden bench in the shade of one of the trees, watching us fight. He looked slightly amused, but I was embarrassed and shoved Trinity a bit suddenly, so she fell off the carpet and on to the ground with a thump.

The man was still smiling, so I smiled back at him. It was another really hot place. The man looked like he'd been out in that hot sun every day of his life. He held a gnarled stick in his hand – he was so old you could scarcely see where the veiny knots on his fingers ended and the knots in the stick began. His robes were long and brown and he wore a white turban-thing on his head. He had the nicest twinkling eyes. I had the feeling that there was some kind of connection between us, one that goes beyond time and space.

I immediately recognised the carpet at work.

Then Trinity made another sudden lunge at me, yelling insults as usual, and, having caught me around the knees unawares, she brought me to the ground. I managed to kick her off as the man said, "Peace, children, peace," in a kind of amused tone. I scrabbled to my feet as Trinity stopped in surprise – she evidently hadn't seen him.

"Peace?" she then spat out, shaking bits of dried up olive tree leaves out of her hair and clothes. "How can there be peace when I live with this idiot of an annoying nerd?" Then she noticed that her hand was bleeding, and the fuss she made of that was unbelievable. She actually accused me of trying to kill her, then swooned and sat on the ground and cried as if in terrible pain. Yeah, right, she didn't even notice the pain until she saw the blood.

I shrugged my shoulders and looked at the man again. He didn't seem to think it odd that we were there. And he seemed to understand. It was kind of nice, because nobody had ever understood before. Most adults I knew would have told me off for hurting Trinity.

The man said to her, with a wink at me, "Are you hurt, my dear? Why not go up to the house – the women will sort out your hand for you."

"OK, I will," said Trinity, tossing her head. "Anything to get away from this idiot fool."

"It's just up the path," added the old man and Trinity stomped off, looking a bit silly in her pink trousers and ankle boots, I thought, but then I probably looked silly in my jeans and T-shirt. We'd have blended in better wearing Christmas nativity play costumes. And that was true for most of the trips, but nobody ever commented – have I said that already? Sorry if I have.

But to get back to where we were. Trinity had gone to check out the house, which you could just catch a glimpse of through the trees, up the hill. The old man smiled and patted the space next to him on the bench, so I went and sat down. It was a beautiful day, though I never did find out where it was. The sky was the bluest blue, with not a cloud in sight. You could only see it by looking up through the olive trees, with their amazing gnarled bark and twisted trunks. A very slight breeze rustled the leaves of the trees and the old man's long white beard.

"She looks like you," he said, after we'd sat there for a few minutes in companionable silence.

"She's my twin," I told him. I wiped my glasses on my T-shirt where she'd grabbed them and made them sticky with her fingers.

"Don't get on, eh?"

"No," I replied.

"Why is that?"

I paused. I'd never thought about that before. We just didn't. But it didn't take me long to decide. After a few moments it all burst out. "She was born first. She does everything first. She has all the friends, all the fun, all the best presents, she's good at everything. Everyone seems to think she's clever and pretty and fun and amusing and she makes them feel sorry for her all the time, when actually she's mean and horrid. People can't see through her! She gets the best of everything, the biggest portion of cake, all the attention and – well, she gets everything and I just get whatever's left over after she's finished. Even our mum's taken in by her."

It was kind of a relief, being so honest. "I hate her," I added. That was the honest truth, too. The man nodded but didn't say anything, and it was like he was giving me permission to say what I really felt. So I carried on. "I feel trapped, like there's no way out. She picks on me constantly. She makes out that everything's my fault when it's not. She helps herself to my stuff, and she's done it since ... well, as long as I can remember."

"I see." The man nodded, a bit sadly. "That's a shame."

"I hate my life," I admitted miserably. "Well, not always," I added quickly, in case it sounded like I was totally depressed. "There's things I really like, but only when she's not around."

The old man nodded again. "What are you going to do about it?"

You know what, I'd never really considered that question – I'd always assumed I'd have to put up with her till we left home. I'd never thought there might be anything I could do. So I thought about it now, with little birds squabbling in the trees above, the insects droning and humming and the warm sun making patterns through the gently rustling leaves.

No point going to Mum, she wouldn't get it. Dad was too far away and who else would care? Our gran thought that the sun shone out of Trinity's ... you know. Spencer was a good friend, but really he just took my mind off the problem for a bit and we had a laugh thinking of awful things we could do to Trinity, which helped for a while until she turned up again.

"I honestly don't think there's anything I can do," I admitted with a sigh.

"You feel powerless," said the man, "because you can't change her."

"That's it exactly," I agreed. "My dad always said that life isn't fair, and I guess it isn't."

"If you can't change the situation, you have to change yourself, and the way you deal with it," said the old man. "You can always choose to do what's right, whatever other people do. God has his purposes in everything that happens to us, both good and bad."

"What purposes?" I asked suspiciously. It's not that I didn't believe him, it's just that it wasn't the answer I was hoping for. I still fancied her getting cut up with a sword, if I'm honest.

"That, lad, we may never know," said the man with a knowing smile, "but we have to have faith. Do you fear God?"

"I've not really thought much about God before," I admitted. No point denying it.

"Well you'd better start thinking," said the man. "You alone are responsible for yourself, and he sees everything."

"If he sees everything, why doesn't he zap Trinity out of my life?" I complained, thumping the ground under the bench with my heels. "I can't be nice to Trinity, it's too hard," I continued lamely, trying to imagine being kind to her and failing. "I'd just be wasting my time because it wouldn't make any difference to anything or anyone."

"It would make a difference to you. I'll pray for you," said the old man. He didn't say anything else, but after a little while I did feel more peaceful. I didn't see how it would make a difference to me, except for being humiliated, but it was a relief just having talked about everything.

Hearing somebody else say that everything wasn't my fault was kind of a new revelation. You probably won't understand that unless you've lived with someone who's made it seem like everything's your fault the whole of your life, gone on at you constantly, bigging themselves up and making you feel small, even if you've done nothing wrong and they have. And in front of other people too. If you have a decent family, you won't get it.

So me and the old man just sat there for a while. I looked around, enjoying the peace of that wonderful place, stashing away all the textures and colours in my mind, so I could add this scene to my selection of paintings later.

After a little while, just as I was wondering if the old man had nodded off, he suggested we walk up to the house and have a drink. I was a bit nervous about leaving the carpet there, but couldn't think of a good reason not to, so we started walking slowly up towards the house.

After a while we met Trinity coming down, her face like thunder. She was stomping and stamping and huffing and puffing the way she usually did when she hadn't got her own way or someone had offended her. I sighed and looked at the old man, thinking I'd have to forgo the drink and go with Trinity, but he made a kind of head nod as if to say, leave her, then smiled in his knowing way, and again that feeling of being understood was so good. So it wasn't all my fault!

Anyway, we let her stomp off and continued our walk up the path, out of the olive grove into the sunshine, which hit you like the heat of an oven when you got out of the shade.

The house was fabulous. It was big and white, like pictures of Greek houses in history books, with pillars in front and a triangular roof, gleaming in the sunshine, and a covered terrace in front running the whole of the width of the house. You know what, when I saw that house, I started to think, wow, I could stay here forever instead of going home! And you don't know what a tempting thought that was.

A smiling grey-haired woman in a Greek toga-like costume welcomed us and helped the man up a couple of steps on to a sort of a patio with pillars in front of the house where there were some more cool white stone benches. We sat down there, and the woman brought us both a smooth, cool drink in a silver goblet. The whole thing was, how can I describe it – better than having ice-cream on holiday in the nicest place you've ever been to, with people you like.

After that the old man suggested that as he was going to lie down for a while, perhaps I'd better go down and check that Trinity was OK? So I set off back down the hill, a bit reluctantly. I'd have liked to have had a look round the house, see what it was like, imagine myself living there.

As I walked, I was thinking of ways Trinity might disappear without me having to do anything to her myself. Perhaps a wild animal would get her, or she might be kidnapped by slave traders, or decide to hitch-hike to Australia.

When I reached the place where we had arrived, where me and the old man had sat on the bench, neither Trinity nor the carpet were to be seen. You know what? My initial thought wasn't panic, it was relief. Perhaps the carpet had made my dreams come true and dropped me off here in this paradise and taken You Know Who away and out of my life for good!

I was just beginning to smile to myself, when Trinity pushed me hard from behind, tripping me up. I landed on my wrist as I fell, which hurt so much I thought I must have broken it. She must have been hiding with the carpet behind a tree, but I was in so much pain I never asked. I could hardly get up.

"That's for trying to murder me earlier," she said through gritted teeth. I presume she meant the scratch on her hand. Murder, I thought, if only I had the courage. Eventually Trinity forced me to roll on to the carpet and off we went.

I hadn't broken my wrist – I spent five hours in hospital with Mum, though, waiting for an X-ray to confirm it. And of course it was my fault, not Trinity's. I tripped over, apparently. Yeah, right.

I really, really regretted leaving that place, and the first person who had ever understood how I felt.

I thought the carpet was getting its revenge for me the next time, though. We went to this awful prison, and Trinity hated it.

seven

The Prisoner

I nearly had the fright of my life when we landed in this stinking, dingy cell, next to a man chained to the stone wall by his ankles. He had long grey hair and a beard, and was wearing filthy rags. The last places we had been to had been like holidays, so this came as a nasty shock.

Trinity started screaming the moment we landed, and I felt pretty panicky myself, which only got worse when a guard came and took the carpet away. He was an enormous man, almost like a giant; his black clothes and grim face added to the terrible atmosphere. He strode into the tiny cell, probably as a result of Trinity's screaming. As he opened the door he let in a bit of welcome light, but he strode straight out again in silence, taking the light and, more importantly, the carpet, with him. He just shook us off it like we were insects.

I tried to get to the door before it closed, but by the time I had picked myself up off the floor, I could already hear the noise of a metal bar being put in place on the other side. It was too awful for words; gut-wrenchingly frightening. The only bit of dim light came from a small, barred hole at the top of the door. The stench was terrible, too, like rotting meat and vegetables. It was so bad I thought I might throw up.

I wanted to say something, but didn't really know what to say – I mean, how can you explain arriving in a prison, with a prisoner already in it? It turns out he wasn't a bad man, but we didn't know that at the time – he could have been a murderer for all we knew. Actually, he was chained to the wall, so he could hardly have done anything to us, whatever he was. Trinity was wailing and screaming, though, and shaking the bars at the top of the door.

The prisoner smiled at me, and I tried to smile back, but believe me, it was terrifying. Eventually, after Trinity had got a bit of a grip (I just stood there, I couldn't think what else to do, apart from try not to vomit from the stench, and I certainly couldn't talk to the man while she was making all that noise), the man spoke. "From whence do you come?" he asked. It was kind of nice to hear him speak normally, in a kind, gentle sort of tone, and not swear or curse or whatever, so I tried to pull myself together. After all, I reasoned, if the carpet had brought us here, it must be for a purpose. Maybe this time I would get revenge on my enemy!

After a bit of a roundabout conversation when neither of us really knew what the other was talking about, we managed to ascertain that we were from afar and he was a prophet from a different place afar.

All this time Trinity was gradually calming down. By the time the prophet and I had worked out that neither of us were ever really going to know where the other was from, Trinity was standing by the door looking angrily at me, hands on her hips. She was breathing heavily, as if it were all my fault we were there, when actually she'd tricked me into getting on the carpet. I didn't tell you about that, did I?

Well, I never wanted to see the carpet again after the olive grove and the wrist incident. It was all too depressing and disappointing, so I chucked the carpet into her room when we got back, and left it there. For several days Trinity had wheedled and moaned and nagged and sulked about going on it again, but there was no way I was going to give in. I didn't want to spend one minute more with her than I had to, and going off on the carpet meant spending time with her. And every single time she had been as nasty as she ever was. Why should I put up with that?

No sane person would choose to spend time with Trinity, I decided.

So, every time she started going on at me, I would go out for a walk, lock myself in the bathroom, or disappear off to Spencer's – anything to get out of her way. But eventually she caught me off guard. She hid the carpet under the throw on the settee, so when I sat down to watch Doctor Who one Saturday evening, she sat quickly down next to me and off we went. I was still fuming when we arrived in the prison. She had laughed all the way, mocking me and making out I was such an idiot to fall into her trap ... but she stopped laughing when we arrived in that prison, as I've already mentioned.

Anyway, back to the prophet – I wasn't sure what one of those was, so I asked him. It's someone who passes on a message from God, he said. Like, God speaks to the prophet, then the prophet gives God's message to the people. Apparently what God has to say is not always well received, and this man had made himself unpopular with some evil rich people, for telling them to stop oppressing the poor. That's why he was in prison.

"You sure that's what God wanted you to say?" I asked. I was thinking, surely God couldn't have wanted it to end up like that.

"Yes," said the prophet, looking very earnest. He wasn't really old; more middle-aged, but his face sort of looked like he had had a lot of trouble in his life. Now my eyes were getting used to the dark I could see he had a really nasty gash down his face, from one eye almost down to his jaw. "God's ways are higher than our ways. We may not understand, but we must still keep trusting him, and be merciful and obedient."

"Oh," I said, wondering how anyone could be talking like that after having had their face cut and been thrown in prison. "Wouldn't you rather get revenge on your enemies?"

He actually smiled. "No, boy, God will judge all things at the proper time." Mm, I thought, that sounded interesting. I liked the sound of God judging. I began to feel more at ease.

"Where did you get that cut on your face? You should have it seen to."

"It was done by a cruel man, who refused to listen to God's message. I'll be honest with you, boy," he said, "I wouldn't have chosen to be a prophet. You don't make a lot of friends. Not many people want to turn from their wicked ways and do good."

"Don't they?" I asked. "Why not?"

He smiled, like I was a bit simple. "Well, boy, most people like doing bad things. They don't want to think about God, because they would have to do what he says and it's much more fun, it would appear, to be greedy and selfish."

"I see," I said, my ears pricking up as I thought of Trinity. I hoped she was listening. She was.

"God doesn't exist, you old fool," she sneered, clinging to the door.

"See what I mean?" said the prophet with a sigh. "Even you, who have come to visit me, don't believe in God and mock me."

"I believe in God," I said, suddenly convinced of it. Trinity smirked, but the man smiled.

"If you believe, turn from your wicked ways and may God have mercy on you, boy."

"What exactly do you mean by turn from your wicked ways?"

He looked at me, and seemed to see that I genuinely did want to know, I wasn't being funny. "When you bring your offerings to God, bring your heart to him, too."

"OK," I said, mulling it over in my mind. I guessed he must mean if you give money to charity, don't do it grudgingly. That made sense. "Anything else?"

"Yes! We must turn away from worshipping other gods. We must give up cheating and stealing, lying and murder and greed. God hates all that. He sees everything. His mercy gives us time to turn from our evil, but for those who refuse to seek God, there will be judgment. Because that's what God's like. He is merciful, but he is also just and fair."

I liked the sound of God being merciful but just and fair. I liked it a lot. Teachers should be like that, I decided. And parents. Then Trinity would get what she deserved.

All this time I had been standing, but I sat down next to the prophet at that point. People had been horrid to him, just like Trinity was horrid to me. I think he appreciated the gesture. The stones felt smooth and cool, and we sat there in silence for a minute.

"What else is God like, as well as merciful and just and fair?" I asked.

Trinity rolled her eyes. "Can't we just go," she said, then kicked the door.

"It was you who wanted to come," I retorted. I was getting used to the stench a bit by then, and my eyes were getting used to the dimness.

Ignoring Trinity, the prophet smiled at me. "What is God like? Bless you for asking, boy. Not many in this land seek after him. He is the only true God! He is the creator of the world. He is the father of our nation, who brought us out of Egypt, out of slavery, to be his own people. He brought us into our Promised Land, where rain falls and dew waits on the ground in the mornings, where there is pasture for the flocks and the herds."

My eyes must have been growing rounder, as I realised he was talking about the time of Elishah and Bildad. "I see," I said, and smiled at the memory of meeting them. "But what do you mean by 'used to'?"

The prophet shook his head sadly. "We refused to follow God's righteous laws, so now we're being slaughtered by foreign armies and taken into captivity."

"Slaughtered and taken into captivity?" I repeated, shocked. "Are you sure?" They didn't teach us that in RE.

"Yes, boy, God brought us into this land, and removed the people who lived here before us because of their wickedness. Now we have become as wicked as them. Some people have even offered their children as sacrifices to gods that are not gods. When people kill their own children, what hope is there? We deserve this judgment."

I sat listening to this in horror. It seemed just too awful. "Is there no hope?" I asked. There had to be hope!

"Yes, my son, in days to come God will restore his people, in his mercy. I see it in my dreams, in a vision of the future. One day our children's children will return here and live in safety." He had tears in his eyes. And then Trinity snorted at me.

"For goodness sake stop listening to all that stupid religious mumbo jumbo," she snapped, "and think how we're going to get out of here, how we're going to get our rug back!"

"Even now, those who seek God will live," continued the prophet, ignoring Trinity and looking at me straight in the eye. "He has sent an enemy to destroy us, but there is still hope for those who turn to him. Even though the enemy is even now at the gates …"

"The enemy's at the gates?" I interrupted in alarm. "Which gates?" I looked towards the door and realised that actually, there was the dim sound of battle outside, and a vague smell of smoke in the air. "Do you mean the enemy is at the gates literally, now?"

"Yes, boy," said the prophet, looking a bit surprised. "Did you not see the vast army on your way in? Listen! Can you not hear the sound of the battle?"

eight

War

I stared at the prophet in horror as put his hand on my arm and said, "Seek righteousness, seek humility. Perhaps you will be sheltered on the day of the Lord's anger."

Well that kind of put the wind up me as you can imagine, especially as just at that moment there was a muffled thundering and shouting coming from outside. "How do we get out?" I asked, stumbling to my feet. I don't mind telling you, my heart was thumping hard.

"The guards will be back soon," said the prophet, as I joined Trinity at the door. "They never let visitors stay long. I appreciate you coming to see me. May Almighty God reward you."

"Um, you're welcome," I stuttered. Trinity was already thumping on the door, yelling to the guard to come and let us out.

The same guard as before came and opened the door for us, but as he did I stepped back to the prophet, who still sat on the stone floor, chained to the wall, tears in his eyes. "Oh my people," he was whispering with his eyes closed. "Why will you not even now turn and live?"

I shook him. "What about you?" I asked him urgently, ignoring Trinity who came up behind me, swearing at me and nearly pulling my arm off.

He smiled a gentle smile, showed me his chains, and said merely, "Go, boy. Do not be anxious for me. God is with me. And remember to show mercy."

By this time Trinity was really hurting my arm and kicking my legs, and I could hear the sound of soldiers and fighting not far off, like in a movie, but way more scary. It gave me serious goosebumps. "You heard what he said, let's go!" she screamed.

We found ourselves in a long, dark corridor with doors leading to cells all the way down, and headed towards a rectangle of light, which we rightly assumed was the exit. Some of the cells had moans coming from behind the bars on the doors, some prisoners were screaming; it was genuinely the worst place I had ever been to in my life, bar none.

We caught up with the guard further down the corridor, near the exit, where I could now see swirls of smoke as well as smell it. You don't get that kind of atmosphere, even in 3D films.

Trinity hammered on the guard's back and yelled at

him, "Where's my rug?" (She swore, but I won't repeat the words she used.)

"He can't reply love, he's had his tongue cut out," replied a man in grey rags from behind the last door in the row, clinging to the bars of his cell. His skinny hand with long finger nails reached out to try and touch us through the bars. His blackened teeth had to be one of the worst things I've ever seen. The guard beckoned for us to follow him through the exit and pointed to the carpet, chucked in a heap on a pile of rubble.

The smoke was so bad by this time you could hardly see a thing – all you could make out were stone walls and people running away screaming and yelling. What with that and the clash and thunder of the battle close by, I nearly froze in terror. Trinity ran straight over to the rubbish pile and started straightening the carpet, yelling at me to help, but I was torn.

"Please let out the prophet," I pleaded to the guard, clinging to his arm. He gave me a large metal key and turned away. I stood holding it for a moment, dithering. I'd like to describe the scene a bit better to you, but all I can remember is confusion, narrow streets and smoke swirling, and people running and shouting and coughing and yelling and bumping into each other. A young woman was screaming, "Joshua!". I don't know if Joshua was her husband, son, cat or dog, but I hope she found him alive.

"Get on the rug!" screeched Trinity, as I turned away and ran back down the corridor we had just come out of. "NOOOOOOOOOW!"

She was almost beside herself by the time I got back from releasing the prophet. As the carpet took us higher, I looked down at the city wall, surrounded by soldiers on horseback and people fighting hand to hand. There were siege machines breaking down the city walls. Buildings were burning – there was the crackle of fire as well as billows of smoke and the shouts and cries of the people who were being slaughtered. I'd lived a sheltered life, I remember thinking.

With a knot of pain in my stomach, as the war-torn city disappeared from view, I thought back to the time of our first trip on the carpet. Elishah and Bildad had been delighted with their new home. Why had everything gone so wrong? God had given his people the land, but was he really now expelling them because they had become just as evil as the people before them? Why didn't they just turn from their wicked ways like the prophet told them to? And what did all this have to do with me?

Trinity disturbed my thoughts. "What a gross, appalling place," she said, turning up her nose. "Why didn't we go to another palace, mix with some decent people, not those filthy prisoners. I need a shower, to wash off the filth."

"It was your choice to go off, I didn't want to," I countered with disgust. As usual, her only thought was for herself.

However terrible it had been, I was glad I had gone. Although the things I had seen had been awful, there was a reason the carpet had taken me there. I knew it. I was beginning to see that life was much bigger than my own little world. And I was beginning to see that there was justice, and there was judgment. I just needed to know how to make them work for me.

nine

Ugly Sisters

Where was justice, I wondered over the next few days, if the prophet was treated like that? The man in the olive grove had said to trust God, but why? What for? What difference did it make? The prophet had said that God would judge, but how would he do that, and when, and why didn't he hurry up? Especially if good people ended up in prison for speaking the truth!

I felt like I had more questions than ever after that trip, and not much in the way of answers. Still, I borrowed a Bible from the school library and started reading it, hoping for more clues. Some of it was interesting. Most of it to be honest I found difficult to understand, but still, it held a certain fascination.

Trinity ignored me for nearly a week after that visit, which was pretty much unheard of, but I wasn't complaining. I thought that maybe, for once, something had happened to stop her thinking about herself, but of course it hadn't. Unfortunately, on our next trip she was back in her element.

Oh, and I forgot to tell you, I found the key to the prophet's chains in my pocket when I got home. After that, whenever I was tempted to wonder if the whole carpet thing was just me going crazy, I got it out and held it in my hand. It was definitely real.

The whole prison thing had made quite an impression on me. The carpet was becoming a bit like an old friend, and I now kept it on my bedroom floor, next to my bed. I often sat on it and thought, and read the Bible, and stroked the patterns and the softness and began to feel that God was with me, in a peaceful kind of way.

I had never thought about mercy before, but the prophet had told me to remember it, so I looked it up in a dictionary. It said, "Kind and compassionate, especially to those who do not deserve it." That made me grind my teeth. I preferred judgment. I still didn't see how they went together, but I felt that I was in possession of several pieces of a jigsaw puzzle, and when I had them all, everything would make sense.

Little did I know what would happen to me next.

We flew off again, totally unexpectedly. Trinity walked into my room unannounced one evening when I was just thinking about going to bed, and as I was already sitting on the carpet, we just took off. Come to think of it, I never did find out what she came into my room for, but she yelled at me the whole journey for being so stupid as to leave the rug on the floor. I mean, where else would you leave it?

This time Trinity loved the place we went to, though. She was totally in her element. She was, at last, she told me later, mixing with people who thought the same way about life as she did. She was totally right about that – the girls there were as mean and nasty as she was.

The carpet had come to rest in warm sunshine at the edge of a garden, where it turned into a vineyard (yeah, grapes growing in bunches on vines, it was awesome!), the sort of country garden you might see in a posh glossy magazine in your dentist's waiting room.

Two celebrity-looking girls in brightly-coloured clothing and loads of jewellery were walking towards us as if expecting us. Well, expecting Trinity.

"Darling, you can't wear that," one said straight away to Trinity, as she stepped off the carpet in her jeans. They swept her away towards an amazing looking manor-type house up a little hill. They totally ignored me, but I didn't mind. Good riddance!

It was another beautiful, sunny place, and for a few minutes I just stood and breathed in the clear, warm air and took in the blue sky and amazing view. Although it was March at home, it had been pretty grey and wet in London, so it was good to feel the sun's rays on my face.

The most incredible flowers and bushes and trees filled the garden, many of which were exotic and I didn't recognise. It was kind of like the King's garden, but ... how can I describe it ... more open and country, less formal and landscaped. More like a parkland than a garden.

There was an older man on his knees doing some weeding in the row of vines next to the bushes, and he signalled to me to come over to him, so I strolled over. A couple of middle-aged, very posh and fancy women walked past me, sounding like they were having a good moan about something. The gardener shrunk out of their way behind the bushes until they had passed. They looked at me down their noses – when the gardener emerged from the bushes he told me we weren't supposed to be seen when the women walked by!

Anyway, the gardener gave me a wooden fork sort of thing and I suppose he thought I was there to help, so I thought why not, and got down on my hands and knees and gave him a hand with the weeding.

I'd never done any gardening before and hadn't got much of a clue, but it was easy enough, copying what the gardener was doing. I thought back to my idea of being a landscape gardener and decided I might as well get in some practice!

After a while Trinity turned up with the girls. When I say girls, I don't mean little kids, I mean teenagers. Dressed to kill for their time, I'm sure. Fancy long dresses, silly things dangling from their hair, covered in jewellery. And make-up – talk about black eyes!

Personally, I prefer girls who look a bit more natural, but hey, these two weren't out to impress me. Far from it. When one of the girls saw me she indicated crossly with her hand for me to get out of her sight. "Don't look at me, peasant," she hissed. I thought she looked totally ridiculous, in shades of pucey-pink, and was quite happy to turn away, but Trinity smirked and said, "Look at me!" So I looked back.

"You know him, darling?" asked the puce girl, turning up her nose as if I was a filthy pig or something.

"Kind of," admitted Trinity, doing a twirl for me to see all her fancy stuff. Actually, she looked totally stupid, but who was I to say? Even Mum would have had something to say about her going out with make-up like that. But as usual, I said nothing – always the best policy if you don't want to get your head bitten off.

"He shouldn't be here when we are. Get out of the way, slave," said the other one crossly. She reminded me of a yellow and green snake.

"Yes, get out of the way, slave," repeated Trinity loftily, turning away.

"Actually, since you're here, you can make yourself useful and bring us some wine," said the puce girl.

"Yes, wine, straight away," gloated Trinity in her annoying way, snapping her fingers in my face.

"We'll be on the swing," said the snake girl. "Well, get to it, slave, I'm thirsty now, what are you waiting for?"

The girls walked off towards a group of trees and Trinity turned and looked at me. "Well, what are you waiting for, slave?" she said, pointing at me with a massive grin. "Hurry up and get me my wine!"

ten

Off With His Head

Now I knew why the gardener had slunk off. I turned to find him, thinking I'd just ignore the girls, but the gardener was wringing his hands. "Quick!" he urged me. "Run up to the house! What are you standing there for? They'll have your head off if they don't get their wine quick!"

I frowned. "I don't even know where the kitchen is, and anyway, I'm not their slave!"

His eyes nearly popped out of his head. "What are you doing here then?" he asked. He had a point. No prince had whisked me off the carpet to dress me in finery. Just as well, I'm not into fancy clothes.

"Anything they want, you need to get it right away, mate, take it from me. Run!" said the gardener, urging me towards the house. He was becoming so agitated, he started to hop from foot to foot.

"But where am I supposed to get it from?" I objected. "I've never been here before!"

"Look, I'll take you," said the man, grabbing my arm and heading for the house at a pace. He looked back anxiously towards the girls, who seemed to have settled on some kind of swing arrangement on a tree, looking like ugly sisters in their stupid clothes.

"Thanks," I said, and had to more or less run to keep up with the gardener as he hot-footed it towards the house. He seemed massively relieved as we approached the house, to see what looked like a servant in posh livery carrying a tray towards us, with three goblets and a jug.

"Wine for the misses?" asked the gardener, sounding like a huge weight had been taken off his shoulders.

"Indeed," replied the servant, a bit loftily. It seemed that gardeners weren't good enough even for him!

"Thank God," breathed the gardener, wiping his sweaty face and hands with a bit of old rag. "If you hadn't come then, I don't know what we'd have done."

Leaving the other servant to carry the tray to the girls, the gardener and I went back to our weeding. Over the course of another hour or so we filled several baskets with weeds, which we emptied on to a compost heap at the end of the row of vines. It was hot, thirsty work in the heat, but I decided that I definitely liked gardening. The brown earth crumbling in my fingers smelt of freshness and cleanness, richness and honesty. And looking back at the bit we had cleared was immensely satisfying.

Grapevines are amazing, too. Have you ever seen vines close up? I guess it must have been spring there, or summer, because tiny new grapes hung in neat bunches, soaking up the sun, next to lush and vibrant green leaves. Little twirly bits coming out of the stems curled around posts. I decided I would definitely have vines in my gardens, when I was a landscape designer!

After a while I asked the gardener what the people here were like to work for. I can't say they had made a favourable impression on me. "Same as with all the posh nobility round here," he said, sticking his fork in the ground as if he wished he was sticking it into one of them. "One foot wrong and you're in prison or in the grave, then your family starves to death. That happened to my brother. Now I've got his kids to feed too." The man stopped for a moment, a stricken look on his face. "We all try to help each other, in the village, but there's a limit to what anyone can do against the power of the rich and mighty."

I must have looked shocked. I certainly felt it. The gardener stopped and looked at me in the eyes. "You're not from round here, are you?"

I shook my head. "No, I come from the south."

"Right, well, God help you, lad. You've got a thing or two to learn."

"What do you mean?"

"Well, you won't get paid. I don't know what they told you, but they'll always find a reason not to pay your wages. And the hours are so long you won't get a chance to grow your own food, or tend your own fields."

I was aghast. "But if they don't pay you, why do you work for them?"

He looked over at me, fierce anger in his eyes. "Because if we don't do what they say, they set fire to our houses, and our crops, saying they have vermin, or any such excuse, just to keep us under, like."

"That's terrible!"

The man nodded. Then the anger in his eyes went out and he seemed to shrink in despair. It was like a wave of hopelessness. "They take our children to be their slaves – our daughters to work in their houses and our sons to work in their fields. We have nothing left but our lives. Our only hope is that God will see us and hear our prayers, and free us from this terrible bondage."

God again! At first I smiled.

"It's nothing to smile at," declared the gardener indignantly.

"Yes, yes, I mean, no, no," I replied hurriedly. "I was smiling because I met a prophet a few days ago and he said that God is merciful, just and fair. I'm sure God will bring justice for you, too." Even as I said it, I felt sure I was right, which is kind of creepy when you hear about our next trip, but I shouldn't confuse you, this one wasn't anything like over yet.

The man sighed. "But how long must we wait?" he groaned, as he went back to his weeding. "We had a prophet travelling round here recently, warning the rich people to stop oppressing the poor. The rich people won't stop their cruelty, though. They like their rich lives too much and need slaves to do everything for them. Good man, that prophet was, spoke the truth, though they threw him in prison for it."

I suddenly had a thought. "He didn't have a long cut on his face, did he?"

"Yes! Nasty gash, from just under his eye, right down to his chin. He was lucky to get away with his life. Not the same one you met then?"

I nodded in surprise. "Sounds like it."

"Well I never! That cut on the prophet's face, the master of the manor did it himself, took his sword to him, he did. Most people bow and scrape to the master, but the prophet stood up to him and told him the truth. He didn't like it. Cruel man, the master is." He nodded his head in the direction of the house.

I was deep in thought as we worked together along the rows between the plants, and my heart was beating hard. How incredible that we had met the same prophet! I thought about the carpet, and wondered about its message for me. I thought about the disgraceful way these people were being treated by the cruel master in the big house, and those awful girls. Strong similarities there with my own life. I lived with my own personal bully/enemy. So was God going to bring me relief from my enemy if she didn't change her ways? Was God going to bring relief for the gardener and his friends, too?

And then I had a sudden thought. The army and the fighting! "How long was it since the prophet left?" I asked the gardener.

"Not much more than a week, I wouldn't have thought."

"Then the army could be here any time!"

"A foreign invasion you mean? Like the prophet told us?" The man paused and shook his head in sombre thought. "There have been rumours of armies approaching from the north."

"You must be prepared," I said in alarm, remembering the cries and the smoke. "The army was burning the city when I was there, but if you do what is right, and seek God, maybe you will be kept safe in the day of the Lord's anger."

After this speech, which astonished me as much as it astonished the gardener, we looked at each other as if seeing each other for the first time.

71

"Where are you really from?" he asked.

"We're from a long way away," I admitted.

"We?" he said, looking round. "Who's with you?"

"My sister, Trinity – she's the girl they dressed in purple when we arrived."

The poor man couldn't take it in. I couldn't blame him really. "So are you a prophet, too?" he asked, scratching his head.

"No, not me," I said with a grin. I didn't bother to tell him I was a schoolboy. "But I visited the prophet in prison and he told me all that."

"He said all that to us when he was here, too," said the gardener. "We used to have a shrine to the god Baal, and our women used to make cakes for the goddess Astarte, but we've got rid of all that now and pray only to the God of heaven, the God who brought our fathers out of Egypt and through the desert to this, our Promised Land."

I nodded, thinking of Elishah and Bildad. How long ago that seemed now! I gave a warm smile and the gardener smiled back.

"It's all very well talking, mate, but we must work or we'll be for it," the gardener said suddenly, going back to his weeding.

"I'm thirsty," I admitted. "Is there anywhere we can get a drink?"

"Not till the sun goes down," he replied.

I was just about to make an exclamation about this when the girls came mincing back in their ridiculous way. One of them had bells on her skirt. It was the stupidest thing ever. All three of them were fluttering their eyelashes and pretending to bow low to someone, mocking whoever it was, and falling about laughing as they went along the path.

I carried on gardening, realising too late that the gardener had disappeared, and that I should have disappeared too.

"YOU!" said the yellow and green snake girl, her vicious eyes full of hatred and her mouth curled up in a sneer. "Get out from our sight!"

"Yeah, get out from our sight!" giggled Trinity and she fell about laughing with the puce girl.

I turned to leave and push through the bushes into the next row, out of sight, as I assumed the gardener must have done without me noticing. He must be well expert at it, I was thinking, I hadn't seen him go, when Trinity called me back.

"What have you done with my rug, thief?" She giggled and was trying not to fall over. It looked like she had drunk too much wine. I fleetingly wondered what Mum would think, but I ignored her. The snake girl pulled herself up to her full height, though, before I could make myself scarce.

She made me realise the saying that beauty is

within is absolutely right, and she was ugly. She was absolutely covered in expensive-looking clothing and jewellery but you could hardly have seen a more hideous, twisted look on her face, which emanated from the evil within. "Give my friend back her rug," she hissed. I almost expected a forked tongue to appear out of her mouth.

"I'm not sure where it is," I answered truthfully, looking round for it. It had to be here somewhere; we hadn't gone far.

"How dare you answer me back," hissed the snake girl. "Get on your knees and apologise or I'll call for the guards to take off your head!"

What would you have done? Humiliating or what? I just shrugged and walked off, intending to find my gardener friend.

"Off with his head," shrieked Trinity as I walked away (she'd watched Alice in Wonderland way too much when we were younger).

And then pandemonium broke out. A whole bunch of guards or troops or something appeared as if from nowhere and grabbed me by the arms. They held scary looking spears, and with the shock I must admit to crying out. The guards held me in a vice-like grip as the snake girl hissed again. "Throw him in the cell!"

"Trinity," I appealed, "For goodness sake tell this witch to let me go."

Well of course that did it. "Witch?" screamed the snake girl. She looked like her head could have blown off in her rage, which shook her whole body. "You called me a witch?"

Trinity began to laugh. "Oh Paul, you are so utterly, stupidly stupid," she giggled. "Oh help, I need a pee or I'm going to wet myself ..."

"Tell them I'm your brother," I pleaded.

"He's my brother," she said, but just as the guards were beginning to relax their grip and I was beginning to breathe a sigh of relief, she added, "but off with his head anyway!" At this, the guards clamped down even harder and I was taken off, yelling and screaming.

They threw me in a dungeon.

eleven

Dungeon

The last thing I remember was being bundled down a stone staircase and the guards chucking me into a dark cell. I must have blacked out – probably hit my head as I landed.

I'm struggling to find words to express how I felt when I woke up. The very first sensations were stiffness, the pitch darkness, and an incredible thirst. Fear didn't kick in until a second or two later.

Writing about it now still gives me goosebumps. I was lying face down on the stone floor. My bad wrist was throbbing really badly (the one that got hurt in the olive grove) and my knees were killing me where they had scraped on the hard stone. My whole body ached and my head hurt. I made it to a sitting position, then realised it wasn't quite pitch black; a faint glimmer of light came from underneath the door. I crawled to it and sat against it, which, being wooden, was slightly less hard than the stone floor. I don't mind telling you that I was really, really, really scared.

After another few moments of sitting there in the dark (this is probably taking longer to tell you than it took at the time), with only my thoughts for company (mostly panicky) I began to get a grip. OK, this was bad, but they hadn't taken my head off yet, and my glasses weren't broken. Trinity couldn't get away without me because the carpet wouldn't work for her on her own – that could be good or bad, depending on whether she wanted to leave or not. It looked like she was in her element, so maybe she wanted to stay. It made me grind my teeth to think of her having a good time, drinking wine, having fun, while I was here, dying of thirst, because of her.

Once my heart had stopped thumping so hard, I decided to grope round my cell. Knowing is better than not knowing, was my reasoning. Once you know something, you can get used to it, or learn to live with it, or find a way to deal with it, or whatever, but while you don't know something, you can't sort it out in your mind. That's how I feel about things anyway.

So I got myself into a kneeling position then cautiously felt around without actually moving to begin with, then I shuffled round on my knees, feeling the walls, then got up and felt the ceiling. The whole thing was about three metres square, high enough to stand in, and I was alone. Very, very alone. I tried calling out, but the thick walls muffled my voice and there was no reply. No sound of anything at all. Here I was, hundreds of miles and hundreds of years away from home. Nobody but Trinity knew I was there, and she didn't care. I started to wonder if I would die there, and if so, how long it would take.

I tried to take my thoughts off dying, and being so thirsty, and my head throbbing, then the prophet suddenly came to mind. He had been in a prison just like this! And he had chains on his feet, too, which would have to be far worse. So for a brief moment I felt kind of grateful. Then I thought how stupid it was to be grateful, when I might die of thirst soon, or be beheaded later, or have to stay in that dungeon till Trinity wanted to go home, which could be months or even years, and wondered if it would hurt if they beheaded me, or if I'd feel nothing, or if they'd put a bag over my head while they chopped … then I decided that I had better think of something more positive than that.

At first I couldn't think of anything much, but after a while I decided to pray, like the prophet had. I started by saying, "Well this is a mess," and that made me smile, partly because it was a relief to hear a human voice (albeit mine) and secondly because it reminded me of Laurel and Hardy, which I used to watch with Dad sometimes in the holidays.

After that I must have rambled on for a while. I just talked. I talked about how I'd got there – about Trinity being swept away by the puce girl and the snake girl, then meeting the gardener. I had a moan about the dreadful way the girls treated people, especially me, and especially Trinity, and wondered if the carpet was still where we had left it. Then I remember asking if God would please sort everything out for me, because it was really horrid in there and I did need a drink badly.

When I stopped talking, I felt a sense of God being there, like I had at home when I'd sat on the carpet with the Bible. I remembered that the man from the olive grove had said that he would pray for me, which felt kind of nice. And then I must have fallen asleep, or blacked out again.

I'd like to say that I was released straight away when I woke up, but I wasn't. I was totally gasping for a drink and was getting feverish by the time two guards came and frogmarched me to the garden. I think I must have drifted in and out of consciousness for hours. My joints were stiff from being on the hard stone floor, my head still hurt and I was so, so thirsty.

Anyway, they marched me to the garden, half dragging me 'cos I could barely walk. I was surprised to find that it was light; I must have been in that cell all night or maybe even two nights, there's no way of knowing. Trinity was wearing some fancy new outfit and was carrying a bag full of stuff – I can't remember exactly what, but she was alone. She said imperiously to the guards, "You can leave him there," which they did, giving me a big shove on to the path, which really hurt my back. As if I didn't already have enough pain everywhere else.

I couldn't get up, but the carpet was there right next to Trinity, so I crawled on to it. Trinity stepped on it and we went home. By the time we got back she was in her old top and jeans, same as me, and no longer had the bag, so I don't know how that worked, but I was so thirsty, stiff and tired and perhaps a bit feverish that I didn't care. I don't know why she wanted to go home – I can only assume she couldn't live without her celebrity magazines, telly, phone and laptop.

When I was back in my room I gulped down the glass of water by my bed (water had never tasted so good!) and Trinity, amazingly, went and brought me up another glass, which she gave me without a word, then I went and filled the glass up from the bathroom, had a pee, yelled goodnight to Mum and went to bed.

That was it, I decided when I woke up next morning, I would never, ever go on the carpet again. Like, never, ever, ever. It was beautiful and I wanted to keep it, but I decided that I'd put it in my wardrobe and get it out every now and then and take a look, but only when Trinity was out. That way we couldn't go anywhere by accident.

So I rolled up the carpet and put it away.

Trinity asked me how I was, the next day after that trip. At first I thought that a miracle had happened. When she came into my room and said, "How are you?" I was sitting on my bed, playing some game, I forget which one now, League of Nations or something, and I lost a life because I stopped to stare at her.

"Um, I'm OK," I replied after a moment's stunned silence. "Back hurts a bit." I winced as I moved. "And my wrist, and knees."

"No need to overdo it," she retorted, so I went back to my game. Waste of time being truthful, I thought. Or talk at all. Why bother?

"I know that wasn't the best trip for you," she said.

"No, it wasn't," I agreed, without looking up. Understatement of the year, I thought, but didn't say it out loud.

"But at last I felt that I belonged somewhere."

"Oh, right." With those awful girls, I thought, that makes sense, but managed to bite my tongue.

"What have you done with the rug?" she asked.

"Why do you want to know?"

"Because." Silence while I played on and she stood there in the doorway, her arms crossed.

"Well if you don't tell me I'll just look."

That wasn't worth considering, I knew she would carry out her threat. "It's in the wardrobe."

"Why have you put it there?"

I thought about my answer to that carefully. If I told her the truth, would it matter? Probably not, I decided, so I told her that I had had enough of adventures, and if it was out of the way, we couldn't go anywhere by accident.

"Why the wardrobe?" she asked.

"I'm not exactly stacked out with space in here."

She nodded. "True."

I nodded back, one eye still on the game, which I was by now losing. Hey ho. That she had agreed with a decision of mine was quite incredible. It was at that point that the conversation disintegrated, though. "I don't ever, ever want to go off on the carpet again," I told her firmly. "So if you were thinking of having any more adventures at my expense, forget it."

She pursed her lips. "They haven't all been bad."

I nearly retorted, "not for you," but actually they hadn't been all that bad for me either. I remembered the camaraderie and optimism of the soldiers we had met on the first trip, that amazing walk in the King's garden (until Trinity had spoilt it), the chat with the nice old man in that beautiful olive grove, where I could happily have stayed, even meeting the prophet in the dungeon, and being able to help him.

That had been good. And I had learned a lot from the gardener, too.

Trinity brought me back to the present with a thump. "Can I have the rug in my room?"

I really didn't want her to have her way and for once I felt a bit bold, with her having agreed with me. "No."

"I'll just take it then."

It was game over on League of Nations or whatever it was. I looked at her. She looked mean, as if a bit of the snake girl had rubbed off on her. I didn't know what to say. "Please don't," I managed. I know that sounds wimpy, but you don't know Trinity as well as I do, or had to put up with her for as many years as I had.

"You get it out, or I'll get it myself," she said calmly, taking a step towards the wardrobe. Bearing in mind that it was only two steps to the wardrobe, she was already half way there. I considered my position. My back still ached and my wrist still hurt from where I'd been thrown into the cell. She was the one who had got me put there. She had talked to me like I was nothing, and told the guards to chop off my head. She might have been messing about, but they could still have done it. Why should I get the carpet for her, why should she have it at all?

So I told her that, and as I spoke my voice got louder and louder as I let off my anger, and she screeched insults back at me, until Mum came up and yelled at us both to shut up. Trinity went off in a huff, Mum slammed the lounge door, and at last I was left in peace.

I could hardly believe it – Trinity hadn't got what she wanted! It felt good, until next morning when I went to my wardrobe to get out a shirt for school.

The carpet was gone.

twelve

Freedom

I'm guessing that because I'd said that I was never going to go off on the carpet again, Trinity made it her mission to trick me on to it. It was either that, or she wanted to go somewhere where she could live for the rest of her life in luxury with servants. But she couldn't get there without me. More's the pity. I could think of nothing better than for her to disappear off to a faraway land, even if it did mean losing the carpet.

She really needed to get a life. Tiresome isn't the word for it. She went on and on and on, nagging and nagging and nagging, days on end. I forget exactly how long it lasted. I so badly wanted to get the carpet back. I missed it. It was like an old friend. I missed the texture, the patterns, and just having it. It had become something special to me, not quite like Bilbo Baggins and his precious ring, but still, I thought about it a lot and wished that Trinity didn't have it.

I nearly gave in once, when she promised she'd give it back if I went on it with her one more time, but I remembered just in time that she never keeps her promises. And I still had that nagging feeling at the back of my mind that she might try to get rid of me if we went somewhere that suited her and she wanted to stay.

I don't know where she kept the carpet. I searched her room when she was out, but didn't find it. I tried the garage and the loft and the shed, and even in our mum's room, under the settee and the sideboard, in just about every single place I could think of, but it didn't seem to be anywhere. It must have been in the house somewhere though, because at times she'd get it out and goad me with it, particularly in the evenings when Mum was out with Laurence.

Anyway, to cut a long and tiresome episode in my life short, she finally got me. I went into the kitchen for a drink one evening and stepped on to it, well, tripped on to it, and she leapt out from behind the door and jumped on it and off we flew.

I said nothing. What would be the point? Like always, I just sighed, and as usual, she gloated and punched my arm and ha ha ha-ed, but I didn't retaliate, just tried to duck her punches. To be honest I didn't dare fight back, because if I had, I could have really hurt her. Not that I couldn't have before, physically, but this time I really felt like I could do something nasty to her. It was getting to the point where I really wanted her out of my life. It wasn't just this last episode with the carpet, but what with that and having lived with her for the whole of my life, I wanted her gone.

It was during that ride that I made up my mind that I would get my revenge. Up until that point I had always put up with her – you'll have seen that by now. But as she punched my arm and gloated about me being rubbish compared to her brilliance, and how she would always be the winner and I would always be the loser, I thought of the kind old man in the olive grove and knew that it wasn't true. He had said to me, "What are you going to do about it?" and I hadn't known. Now I knew.

I didn't know how I would do it, but revenge would be sweet, I thought, as I sat there on the carpet, dodging her punches. I had been merciful long enough. Now, I decided, was the time for justice, and judgment. I decided to ask Spencer for advice, assuming we got home. He'd be glad to help, and he had a lot more imagination than me.

Anyway, thoughts of revenge had to be shelved for a while, as we swept down to a hillside on a lovely summer's day. It was the shortest and simplest of the trips we ever went on, but by no means the least instructive.

We didn't meet anyone else the whole time we were there. The carpet alighted on a scrubby area in front of a ruined mansion. Everything that had been made of wood was burnt and charred, the stone walls were crumbling and blackened, and weeds were taking over where there had once been a courtyard and a garden beyond. A big black bird sat on one of the higher bits of broken wall and cawed – I'm not very good on birds, but I think it might have been a crow. The sound sent shivers up and down my spine. Actually, it still does now, when I think of it.

Apart from the bird, the whole place looked completely desolate and overgrown. And then it dawned on me. Yes, you've guessed it, it was the same place we had come to the last time.

I ran down the slope to where I would have walked up the path with the gardener – I passed the place where we met the servant with the tray of wine for the girls, and on down to the vineyard where I had done a bit of weeding with the gardener. There was no doubt about it, this was the same place, but some time later. Nettles and thorns covered the vineyard I had weeded with the gardener, and big bunches of grapes were rotting amongst the weeds.

Sombrely I walked back up to the house, remembering with feeling being dragged there by the guards. Ignoring Trinity, I went to look for the dungeon they had thrown me into and found it, still half underground. It felt strange going in, through a broken-down archway and down some crumbling stone steps.

The door to my former prison was now hanging badly on one hinge. The rough stone on the ground where I had hurt my knees was still there, though – I rubbed my hand over it, then over my knees, which had now healed over. It was kind of creepy.

I sat down, with my back to the doorway, where I had sat not that long ago. I tried to remember if I had been wearing the same clothes. The jeans were probably the same. It was no longer pitch black in there, due to the walls being broken down, and the atmosphere was no longer frightening and I was no longer on death row, but still, it was the same place.

I wondered what had happened. Perhaps the foreign army had come and burned down the house. That seemed the most likely explanation. I heard the crow caw again. I wondered if the gardener had escaped with his life. I hoped so. I thought about the words I had spoken to him – well, the words of the prophet that I had repeated to him, that God would come to their aid.

It seemed like justice had been done. I went back up the steps and back into the sunshine, which felt so, so good.

I sauntered back up to the main level of the house. Trinity was wailing as she wandered around the ruins, having made the same connection as I had between her new "friends" and what was now left.

But I felt more cheerful than I had for a very long time, perhaps ever! I don't know if you can understand this, but I felt free, maybe for the first time in my life.

Lizards were sunning themselves peacefully on the ruined stones and some birds were nesting in a bush that had grown over one of the walls. It was so wonderful – I wish I'd had my phone or camera with me so I could have recorded it, but I made some mental pictures, so I could paint them in my own time when we got home. While Trinity was wailing and crying and bemoaning the lot of the people she had "felt the most at home with, *ever*," I planned my paintings of this place. I would do a before and after! What a victory for justice!

The sun was shining brightly, and it was such an awesome day in so many ways. The glorious sun, the scent of fragrant blossom in the air, the delicious greens of the gloating plants were a delight to the soul. Excuse the poetry, but it really was amazing! I ran my hand over the ruined wall, so I would remember the texture and be able to give it life when I painted it.

I was glad Trinity had tricked me into going there – I was really enjoying it and she was really hating it! Ha ha, I thought, well that would serve her right!

Then of course she wanted to go home, before I was really ready to go. I sighed. Her eyes were swollen and red and puffy, and she looked kind of crestfallen, not like her usual crowing self.

"So, glad we came?" I asked, all innocent, not.

"Of course," she spat out, flicking her head at me.

"I found the dungeon you got me thrown into," I told her airily, as if I was telling her about a hotel room I had stayed in once. "Care to take a look?"

For once she looked horrified, just for a second. "No."

"Why not? It's not pitch black any more, now the walls have been broken down."

"I said no."

I shrugged. "Suit yourself, but you're missing out on an experience." I don't know what made me so daring. I think it was that at last I was enjoying myself at her expense, not the other way round. Perhaps for the first time in our lives.

"I want to go home," she repeated petulantly.

"Well I don't, so you'll have to wait for me." Get me, being that bold. I could scarcely believe my own words and I don't think Trinity could either, but I walked away before she could retaliate with something caustic. But she didn't even call any insults after me, she just sat on a broken stone wall and cried.

To be honest, I didn't really enjoy the rest of the walk after that, but I made it last a bit, just to show her. Then I walked back to the carpet where Trinity was waiting for me, and we flew silently home.

I'd never really had a chance to think much about the journeys before, as we'd always been fighting, but I decided when I started painting the images, to add a picture of the carpet flying too, perhaps with me on it, but without Trinity. It didn't fly completely flat, it kind of curled up and down at the edges a bit, like a manta ray gliding through water, sometimes like a bird soaring, sometimes "flapping" a bit more than that. But it was always very gentle. And strangely, you couldn't really see what was down or around, once you were up, it was always misty and dim. Apart from once, but I'll tell you about that later.

I thought after that ride we wouldn't be going anywhere else. That would be that, I thought. Neither of us would want to go now, and actually, for a while, Trinity did give it a rest, and I started painting.

It was a wonderful couple of weeks, perhaps the best in my whole life up till then! The feeling of freedom that I had felt in the ruins had kind of rubbed off – it was amazing.

I only painted when You Know Who was out, but as it was Easter holidays, I had plenty of time. I had to paint at the dining table, but that was fine, I could spread out, and as Trinity was out a lot with her friends, that wasn't much of a problem. When she was in, I sketched in my room, planning, working on the outlines, the perspective, who and what I would include and leave out.

It was amazing, like this was what I was born for. I either painted or sketched, hours on end. Mum was pleased, I think she saw how much I was enjoying it. She didn't know how little exam revision I did though!

The paintings gradually took shape, out of my mind and on to canvas, of the places we had been to and the people we had talked to. I did the pictures in the order we had done the trips.

I started with the soldiers on the hillside, with that amazing view in the background and the girls at the well. Elishah was the main focus of the painting, showing moves with his sword, with Bildad looking on, arms folded, smiling. It was a triumphant picture and I was really pleased with the way I caught the light glinting on the blade, and the jewels on the hilt. I called it "The Overcomers". The title came to me as I was finishing – it seemed kind of appropriate. It was like, they had ousted the child sacrificers, then got to live in their Promised Land after living in the desert. That had to be good. I wondered if I would ever get to be an overcomer myself, and had that feeling deep down that one day I might. That was jigsaw puzzle piece one.

The next picture was the King in his garden. I was really pleased with the way the fountain sparkled, the way the shadows melted over the bushes and walls and trees, but in the sunlight the colours were vibrant on the plants and bushes through the archway, just as it had in real life. I wasn't sure what to call that one for a while, but I decided on "Authority" in the end, because people's lives depended on the King, and supposedly on me, too.

The third painting was of the old man in the olive grove, which I did mostly in gentle shades of green. There was a real peace and softness about that one. I called it "Understanding".

After three "nice" pictures, the atmosphere in the next one was completely different. I painted the prophet chained to the wall in his cell, mostly in shades of grey and brown. I used long, hard strokes, to convey the horror of his unjust imprisonment, and that's what I called it in the end, too: "Injustice".

Lastly were the "before" and "after" paintings of the mansion garden we had visited. In the first one I wanted to get over the horribleness of the place, but as I sketched the girls in that beautiful garden, it didn't really work out, because outwardly everything looked lovely! After many ideas and deletes, in the end I settled for head and shoulders of the two horrid girls' faces (puce girl and yellow-and-green snake girl), with the gardener working in the vines in the background. The girls were looking at each other, sneering in what I hoped showed their inside nature.

As a last minute inspiration I added a row of barbed wire as a border all round the painting, to symbolise the oppression and slavery. Even that didn't give exactly the impression I was looking for, so decided to add a picture of me as a dark shadow in my prison in the lower right quadrant of the picture, and that made all the difference. I called it "Evil".

Then I painted the ruined mansion with the crow, and lizards on the broken stones and called it "Freedom", with my dungeon cell as it was the second time, empty, when it was a ruin. I managed to get a shaft of light coming through the broken door, which gave exactly the atmosphere I wanted to convey.

As I painted that picture I could sense the justice in it, and the light and the freedom, and I was glad. I was glad for the gardener and the rest of his people. I was glad for the prophet (who was free, too) and I was glad for myself. And I was glad for the world, that justice existed. The only painting I didn't get round to was the one of the carpet flying, because I couldn't decide whether to put myself on it or not.

I sort of prayed, while I painted, like I had in the prison. Only when Mum wasn't around, of course. Praying is maybe a posh word for it, I just talked really, about how things were. I talked about Dad leaving, and about Mum and Laurence. I told God about Trinity. And I felt that he was kindly listening, and even understanding, like the old man in the olive grove.

thirteen

The Plan

I didn't get to see Spencer until the last day of the holidays because he was away at some camp. When he came round we decided to watch a load of Star Trek episodes back to back, as everyone else was out, but half way through the second DVD we were hungry, so we went and stocked up on snacks before going back to the living room. It was Spencer who brought up the subject of the carpet.

"I don't even know where it is at the moment," I admitted, "but I have been on it a few times." I recapped briefly. His mouth had dropped open by the time I'd finished. Fortunately he knows me well enough to know that I'm not a total nut job. "Actually," I finished, "I'd really like some help getting revenge on Trinity. Justice, kind of thing."

Spencer nodded. What he thought about our adventures I'm not sure, but anyway, he was his usual enthusiastic self. "Revenge would be good," he agreed. "And not before time. How you've put up with her this long I'll never know."

I had to agree. "Got any ideas?"

"Well you could lock her in a garage or a shed or a cupboard or something, see how she likes being locked up. Preferably in the dark and all night. Without food and water. That would serve her right." His eyes were gleaming. After all, he had known Trinity almost as long as I had.

I nodded. That was a possibility. "How would I do that without being detected though? I mean, without anyone knowing it was me. Or anyone letting her out?"

Spencer pursed his lips. "Good point. Ah," he then said, "you could go in her room and smash her stuff, put bleach on her clothes, graffiti her books and furniture and things – I'll help you now if you like, no sweat. It would be fun and a pleasure to help."

I looked a bit askance at that thought. "But they'd know it was us."

Spencer's face fell. "Yeah, I suppose so." After thinking for a minute he came up with what seemed like the best plan yet. "You know you said that once Trinity nearly fell off the carpet, because she was just stepping on to it when you took off?"

"Yeah ..."

"Well, next time you go on it, couldn't you shove her off it?"

I grinned. Sorry, I know that's not very nice, but I'm telling it as it was.

"Try and do it when you're over the sea, or a mountain range or something," Spencer carried on, warming to his theme (I told you he has more imagination than me).

"I'm not even sure we pass over anything like that," I said uncertainly, racking my brain to think of what we did fly over, but coming up with pretty much a blank, apart from immediately as we were arriving at or leaving a place.

"Paul, you're such a nerd sometimes," said Spencer with a sigh. "How come you didn't notice?"

"I dunno," I replied lamely. "Rubbish, aren't I? I can show you where we went, though," I added, suddenly thinking of my paintings.

So we went up to my room, Star Trek completely forgotten, and I got out all my canvases from where they were stacked under my bed.

"Wow," said Spencer. "You are so good at this." Then he saw the pictures of the dungeon, before and after I'd been in it. "Is this where you were?" he asked, his eyes nearly popping out of his head in amazement.

"Yup."

"All night?"

"I think so – it was pitch black in there, so I can't say for sure what the time was when I went in or when I came out. But Trinity was wearing a new outfit when I got out, like she'd got dressed in the morning, and I was dying of thirst, literally, my tongue was all swollen and I could hardly walk, so I think it was at least one night."

"Man, you definitely need to get revenge."

"Yeah, I do. Actually, I like the idea of pushing her off the carpet, I like it a lot."

"So when are you going to do it?"

"I don't know."

"But you will do it, right? And you'll let me know how it goes?"

"Sure," I said with a grin.

"Promise me you won't chicken out?"

"Nope, this time I'm going to do it!" We grinned at each other and high-fived and went back to the telly.

And I did do it.

For once it was me wanting to go on a trip, not Trinity, but following Spencer's advice, I kept it really cool and waited a few days. It's a bit embarrassing to admit that I wasn't thinking about where we might be going on the carpet, or why – I just wanted to see Trinity fall. It became a bit of an obsession. I ended up daydreaming in lessons how I would do it, when we were supposed to be preparing for exams.

Spencer helped my imagination; he had loads of good ideas. I think I've already told you he suggested that I shove her off over a mountain range or an ocean. I couldn't think of anything better than that, but just about every day he came up with a new idea. At the top of a waterfall, so she went over it; over the North Pole so she landed on the ice miles from anywhere; over a herd of elephants so they trampled on her – it sounds silly, looking back on it now, and somehow it never occurred to us that she could actually die. Writing that now, it seems so absurd.

I have to say that I did nearly chicken out, because for a while Trinity left me alone. No "I'm so much better than you" jibes at everything, no snide comments, no laughing at everything I did, no tripping me up deliberately, no sneaking around listening to conversations so she could mock me, no nicking my pyjamas when I was in the shower, no putting salt in my tea, no hiding my school books, no being mean at all. Not even mean looks, which she had perfected to, well, perfection.

I'm guessing that the change in her was the result of the experience of seeing the ruined house. It seemed to affect her deeply. For me, seeing the before and after was a liberating experience, but for her, well, she'd lost her new friends in a pretty dramatic way. For a couple of days I did wonder if she might have taken the prophet's message to heart and had decided to change her ways.

I had Spencer on my back, though, asking when I would do the deed, and as the leaving me alone phase didn't last much more than a week, it wasn't long before my dithering ended.

It was a Tuesday morning. What I did wrong I have no idea, but something must have snapped in Trinity, because she threw my packed lunch on the floor and stamped on it as soon as Mum had gone to work. Then of course it was my fault and the yelling, screaming and everything started just like before. No permanent change then.

So me and Spencer made our final plans at lunch time (he let me share his lunch, he's a good mate). We decided that I would put the carpet down where you walk in my bedroom door (I forgot to tell you, she'd let me keep it this time). I'd call her into my room and be standing on my bed, pointing to something out of the window, as if I was looking at something amazing, like a hot air balloon or something, then I'd leap off the bed on to the carpet before she could get off it.

Spencer made me promise that I would text him just as I was about to put the plan into action – he knew I'd chicken out if I didn't. So that evening, when Mum had gone out, I set up the carpet just inside my bedroom door, opened the curtains, texted Spencer, then yelled, "Wow, look at that!" really loudly. After the third yell, when I was just about to text Spencer to say that it hadn't worked, Trinity stalked in, in a foul mood.

"Shut up!" she screeched, her whole body seeming to screech too. But she had stepped on the carpet, so I more or less fell off the bed on to it, and off we flew.

She was furious. "I was watching *I'm a Celebrity*," she screamed, "now I'm going to miss it and it's all your stupid fault, you stupid nerd, you pointless waste of skin, you pathetic loser, you ugly camel-faced git, you pathetic moron ..." and so she went on, swear words included. I can't remember the exact insults she used, but those are all stock ones, so you get the picture. It was a stupid thing to screech about anyway, because no time ever seemed to pass while we were away. Whatever it was she was watching would still be on the telly when we got back.

I started to push her off straight away, while she was still screaming at me. I had already decided to do that, so I didn't lose my nerve and change my mind. What we were travelling over at the time I have no idea – there was the usual general haze, so I didn't get to pick where I was going to push her off. No carefully choosing the open ocean or mountain range. Waste of planning time, that was. Anyway, I thought grimly, fighting back properly for the first time I could remember (might have done when we were toddlers), anywhere would do.

Embarrassingly, I enjoyed watching the shocked look on her face as I pushed her towards the edge of the carpet. It didn't take much, actually. The best bit (apologies in advance) was that as she rolled off she grabbed the edge with her fingers and I kicked them off, one at a time. Oh what a great moment! Oh the satisfaction! Ha ha ha, I did enjoy it, for about a second. Then of course it all went wrong.

Why me and Spencer hadn't considered this I will never know. The carpet just fell out of the sky. Well it would, wouldn't it – it only flew when Trinity and I were both on it. So for about a second, the carpet kind of hovered and twitched, then it began to fall out of the sky. Downwards. Fast. I remember closing my eyes as I saw the ground coming up towards me – what a shock that was, still, it was worth it, was my last thought before a sudden thud made me open my eyes again – Trinity had landed back on the carpet. How she did it I will never know, but the murderous look in her eyes wasn't nice.

Sigh. Ever get the feeling that nothing goes your way? That nothing is ever going to go your way? Like, never in your life? I had that feeling, and as we landed on the ground in the usual way, I had to run to get away from her. I could have fought back of course, having discovered how easy it was, but something inside me knew that it was pointless. It seemed like

I would never, ever win, however much she ruined my life.

We had landed on the edge of a field of sheep. Without any thought as to where I was going, I leapt off the carpet, vaulted over a stone wall then ran down a grassy path. I just wanted to get away.

fourteen

Hiding

I could run quite a bit faster than Trinity, but I could still hear her shrieking behind me somewhere as I ran round a corner and entered a village that looked like it came out of a Christmas card (except that it was daytime, not dark.) Nobody was in sight. Needing to lose You Know Who, I took a turning to the back of a row of houses, and bumped straight into a man loading vegetables into sacks next to a tethered donkey. Middle aged sort of man, really pleasant face. The sort of man that if you could pick your teacher, you might pick him.

"Whoah," he said, getting his balance. "Running from someone are we?" He was kind of chortling. Chortling is not a word I use often, but he did have a jolly kind of laugh, not a mean one, if you know what I mean.

"Yes," I replied, panting, ducking behind the donkey.

"Who from?" he asked with a grin, indicating a mound of hay I could hide behind. I could hear Trinity making a fuss in the main road somewhere behind us. (I say main road, but it wasn't much more than what we'd call a farm track.) I leaped behind the hay and tried to stop panting so hard. "My sister."

The man laughed again, as if that really amused him. "No worries, son, hide here till she's gone. I'll fend her off if she comes this way!" He carried on packing up his veg and chortled again as if it were all a big game. If only he knew!

It was cooler in the shade behind the haystack and I was glad to stop and catch my breath and take a look around, wondering where and when I was. Chickens were scratching round in the dust, and a goat was tethered to a tree not far away. This man's house (behind which I was sitting) was the last in a row of simple but neat places, made of stone with flat roofs and steps up to the roof. I had certainly travelled back in time, as usual, but how far back I couldn't tell. Not that it mattered.

An old lady in black was sweeping her flat roof with a broom, a couple of roofs down, but I noted with relief that she didn't seem to have noticed that I was there. So as I had lost Trinity, at least for the moment, I sat with my back against the hay and reviewed the situation, as they say in Oliver Twist. I felt a bit like Oliver Twist, too, in a way – downtrodden and in a dangerous place.

I heard Trinity having an argument with someone not too far off, but as the voices started to recede into the distance, then disappear altogether, I began to breath properly again. I had lost her! What a relief that was!

"Mother Marianne has taken her in by the sound of it," said the cheerful man, bringing round his donkey and tethering her to a post. "She'll sort her out." He laughed, so I did too, just to be polite. I didn't feel cheerful, though. In my heart I knew I had made a big mistake. Unless we stayed here forever, I would have to face Trinity again, and there was no way she would ever, ever forgive me for pushing her off the carpet. If things had been bad before, what would they be like now?

"Fancy a bite of breakfast, son?" the man asked. "You can come out now, she's proper gone down the road. Come and meet Anna, my missus, she likes having company!"

There didn't seem any harm in that, so I got up and the man slapped me round the shoulders and led me into his house, where a smiling woman dressed in a brown robe was cutting up hunks of coarse brown bread into thick slabs. Well I'd only had half a lunch (half of Spencer's) and hadn't had tea at that point, so I tucked into breakfast with enthusiasm when they pulled up a stool for me around a table, and handed me a plate with some of the bread and a slab of goat's cheese on it.

Before eating, these people said a thank you prayer. It was kind of neat, like they were truly grateful for having something to eat. They were a well nice couple too, really friendly. While we ate (it was simple, but totally delicious), we talked about nothing in particular for a while, then the man, whose name was Seth, asked me why I was hiding from my sister.

I probably sighed, as usual. I didn't feel like talking about her. The freedom I had felt after seeing the burnt and broken mansion had totally evaporated, and the satisfaction of having pushed Trinity off the carpet had been swallowed up by the aftermath. I now felt trapped and desperate. Even just thinking about it made my stomach churn.

"We were fighting," I managed eventually.

"About what?" asked Anna. "You don't look the fighting sort to me!"

I decided to keep it really simple and hope to change the subject. "She has been horrible to me ever since I remember," I told them. "I was trying to get justice, but actually I think I went about it all wrong. I wish I'd never bothered."

"We all make mistakes," said Seth cheerfully, slapping me on the back again.

"We certainly do!" said Anna, getting up to wash up the plates in a bowl of water from a pottery jug. Gran would have died at the lack of hygiene.

"Fancy taking a walk, son?" suggested Seth. "I need to take an order to the next village with Tiglath today."

"Tiglath is our donkey!" said Anna, laughing at my blank expression.

Now that sounded like a good escape plan. "That would be great, thanks," I agreed with a smile. Anywhere, as long as Trinity wouldn't be able to find me. Even as I was saying that, we heard shouting and yelling from the direction of Marianne's house. Seth must have seen my face fall.

"Don't worry, son, we'll sneak out," he said with a wink and a grin. "Let's go!"

"OK," I agreed, rising quickly to my feet and brushing animal hair off my clothes. I'd had to take a couple of donkey-looking hairs off the cheese. Really, Gran would have had a fit.

"Come with us, Anna?" suggested Seth.

"Sure, I'll finish off clearing up when we get back," agreed Anna. She grabbed a headscarf thingy and off we went.

At first we walked quickly, avoiding the main path, checking over our shoulders to make sure nobody from the village saw us going. Seth and Anna both seemed to be really enjoying being furtive, like it was a fun game – maybe it made a nice change for them from the usual daily tasks. As far as I was concerned, there was nothing enjoyable or fun about it whatever, but as we put in more and more distance from the village with no sign of followers, I began to relax a bit.

"Have you been here before?" Anna asked, as we climbed up a stony hill. It was hard work, and the sun was getting hotter.

Puffing and panting, I was about to say that I didn't think so, but as we reached the top I cried out in surprise. It was the first hill we had come to with the carpet – the hill where I had met the soldiers. This was the same hill they had walked down! "Actually, I have, but it was some time ago," I cried out in amazement, looking down towards the well, and the troughs for the sheep. "I don't suppose you know a Bildad and an Elishah, do you?"

Seth and Anna looked blankly at each other and shook their heads. Hardly surprising really, the soldiers had just been passing through.

It was incredible that I was in the same place, though, and I did feel a bit relieved, as it seemed that whatever terrible decision I had made about pushing Trinity off, the carpet still had everything in control. That was reassuring.

So we stood there, the three of us, enjoying the awesome scene, hills rolling away into the distance.

"I'm so going to do a painting of this when I get home," I said to neither of them in particular – more to myself really. Exactly the same background as the first picture I had painted, I decided, weighing it all up in my eye, but with Seth, Anna and the donkey instead of Elishah and Bildad.

"Our Lord taught us on this hill," said Anna, as Seth took her hand in his. She sighed, a bit like I do, but her sigh had a different meaning. For her, it seemed like a precious memory. For me, a sigh meant that I was beaten again.

I didn't know who their lord was, so I didn't comment. Anyway, if they had a precious memory, I didn't think they would want me interrupting it. So after enjoying the view for a bit, we walked down the hill, following the path as far as a river, then turned to the right along the river bank.

It was deliciously cool under the shade of the trees, after having been out in the open sun. As we got further and further from the village, I began to enjoy myself. Here I was, walking along a river path in the dappled shade with a really nice couple and their donkey, when I should have been doing homework in my bedroom!

To say it was an awesome walk would be an understatement, and I started to feel lighter within myself as we talked and laughed and got further away from Trinity. Seth even let me have a go at leading

Tiglath! I'd never got that close to a donkey before. They have the softest hair and long flicky ears, and you should see the amount they can carry! I could seriously use a donkey to carry my school stuff about, especially on days we need sports kit!

"So you're an artist?" asked Seth when he asked what I liked doing and I told him that I like painting.

"It's the only thing I'm good at," I told him, kicking a stone and sighing. "And I'm the ugly one. My sister's supposed to be good looking, although actually, when she's got one of her faces on she looks ugly too. Which is most of the time."

"I don't think you're ugly," said Anna indignantly, giving me a hug around the shoulders. I wondered if she might take me in, if we didn't go home; she looked about the same age as my mum.

"Anyway, it's what you're like inside that counts," said Seth.

"I agree," I replied with feeling, kicking another stone. And I told them the story of the girls in the mansion who had fancy clothes but were really cruel. I finished with them having had me thrown into the cell without a drink. I could feel their sympathy. It cheered me up a bit. Anna put her arm round me and Seth patted my shoulder.

"So that's why you said you wanted to get justice?" asked Seth after a while.

I nodded. And I probably sighed. You know what, I really, really wanted to tell them about pushing Trinity off the carpet, but I didn't know where to start with that, so I just told them that eventually they had let me out and I went home, but Trinity was still mean. I told them that she had thrown my lunch on the floor and stamped on it, and that I'd tried to get my own back but had failed. Which is why she was chasing me.

"Oh dear," said Anna. She sounded shocked, which any decent person would be. "So what are you going to do now?"

"I don't know," I replied honestly. "I don't want to go home. I can't face her again!"

"Actually, turning the other cheek is one of the things our Lord told us when He was here," said Seth.

If their lord was like the master of the manor who had treated the people really badly, I could do without his advice. "Really?" I said. "I've done that most of my life and it hasn't worked."

"Surely you'll be setting up your own home soon," said Anna with a smile, "so if your sister really is that horrid, you won't have to see her so much. Are you betrothed to a nice girl?"

fifteen

Rich People

The thought of being betrothed made me laugh. As if! "I'm not betrothed at all! Nobody would want me, anyway," I added with a sigh. That was true enough. No girl looked at me.

"Oh dear, we have got a touch of the self-pities," said Seth with a grin, but I didn't grin back.

Anna put her arm round me again. "What makes you think nobody would want you?" she asked.

I shrugged. I just felt that way, but I didn't know how to express it.

"Come on," said Seth in a teasing way. "You look like a great guy to me!"

"I'm a loser," I managed. I know it sounds pathetic, but it was the only way I could think of to express the way I felt at the time.

"What have you lost?" asked Seth with a chortle. I know it sounds like he might have been annoying, but it didn't come over like that, he was just being friendly.

And that made a nice change, believe me.

"I dunno," I sighed. "Just at the moment, I feel a bit lost all over."

"Jesus came to seek and save the lost," said Anna. That made me look up in surprise – time jump or what? Anna mistook my astonishment. "You do know who Jesus is?" she asked tentatively.

"Yes, of course I do," I said with a nod. "Well I've never met him myself," I added hastily, in case he'd actually been around the day before or something. "But I've heard about him. He didn't live here, did he?"

"No, no!" laughed Seth. "He came from Nazareth, although he was born in Bethlehem."

"Oh yes, of course," I said. I did kind of know that.

"We met him once," said Anna, in an awed tone, like she was talking about a celebrity.

"Really?" My mind was working overtime. Jesus was a real person then. Plus, I was thinking this must have been a long time after the time of Elishah and Bildad. Hundreds, if not thousands of years. Could it be that the countryside hadn't changed much in all that time?

Anna nodded. "It was amazing, meeting Jesus. Shall we tell you about it?"

To be honest, at that time I wasn't really that interested in hearing about Jesus, but I decided that the least I could do was to be polite, so I nodded.

And it turned out that Jesus was the next piece in the jigsaw puzzle. To cut a long conversation short, and leaving out Seth's veg delivery because that was pretty uneventful, it turned out that Jesus, who is God's Son, came to tell everyone about the way to heaven. He visited Seth and Anna's village and apparently he talked a lot about justice too! I tell you, my spine was tingling when they told me that. I did get a bit confused when they started talking about the difference between justice and revenge, then added mercy into the mix.

I told them straight, I wasn't up for being merciful to Trinity; it was pointless, until they explained that God would only forgive us if we forgave other people. That sounded a bit daunting, but I have to say that forgiving her sounded vaguely possible at the time, when she wasn't there and with these people in a beautiful place in the sunshine.

We didn't just talk about Jesus, we talked about all sorts of things and nothing in particular as we wandered back to their village along the path by the side of the river, then sat and dipped our feet in the deliciously cool water, in the shade of trees that buzzed with insects. The trees and plants were different to the ones at home, but the sparrows were the same.

Anna said something about the sparrows I will never forget, when I mentioned that I could hear sparrows just like those ones, from my bedroom window. God takes care of the sparrows, she told me; Jesus had said so. He knows about each one, and in just the same way he knows about them, he knows all about me and cares about me, too. I wondered aloud why God would bother with me.

"Each one of us is precious in his sight," Seth said.

"How do you know?"

"Because Jesus said so."

I nodded. If Jesus was God's Son, then what he said would be true, wouldn't it? It was a nice thought that God cared about me. But expecting me to forgive Trinity was a big ask.

We talked and laughed all the way home. Anna told loads of stories – really interesting stories about all sorts of stuff, not just Jesus and God. They both talked about their families (you wouldn't believe how many brothers and sisters they had!), and I told them a bit about my gran and my aunties and cousins. They told me about the time when Jesus was around – amazing, incredible stuff. I'd read some of it in my Bible, but they told me loads more. He did miracles, drove out demons, lived simply, loved everyone he met, and he taught them all about God. It was awesome. My eyes were just about popping out of my head by the time they finished.

They talked about funny things that had happened to them, too – sneaking off together before they were married, Seth pushing Anna in the river by mistake, antics of their animals, Tiglath taking off a tax collector's hat, stuff like that. It doesn't sound funny now, but it was when they said it.

When we got back to the house, I helped Seth with the animals. I brushed Tiglath and put hay in her manger, fed the goats, caught and locked away the chickens in their coop for the night (ever tried to catch chickens? It's hilarious!), milked the goats (well I mostly watched, I was rubbish), then put them all in the stable for the night. The stable was really a part of their home, it was neat – you walked through a door and down a step to the stable, or you could get to it from the outside.

When we went into the house proper, Anna was ladling some sort of stew into wooden bowls. Really good stew it was, a million miles away from the microwave macaroni cheese Mum had left out with a note. It was a really awesome meal in an amazing setting – rustic I think is the word. I felt totally accepted. After the meal we sat in the twilight and talked.

After a while I mentioned revenge again – I can't remember how it came up. Anna got up and lit an oil lamp because it was starting to get dark and Seth said, "Let me tell you a story about Jacob, one of our neighbours. Last year, his goats broke loose. They are always breaking loose. Jacob likes his wine, and doesn't always do things properly when he's been drinking. Well, on this one particular day, Jacob's goats wandered into our house and started eating our blanket. We only have one blanket; now it had holes!"

Anna smiled at the memory and shook her head. "I was so cross, you should have seen me chase those goats out!"

I smiled back. "So what did you do?"

"We had a choice," said Seth slowly. "Me and Anna talked about it when I came in from the fields. We could get justice – ask Jacob to replace the blanket, or we could exact revenge – get our goats to eat Jacob's blanket!"

I laughed. "You didn't do that, though!"

Seth's eyes glinted in the light of the lamp flame. "No."

"So you went for justice?"

Seth shook his head. "No, we decided not to do that, either. We forgave."

I nodded in the silence. Anna took Seth's hand across the table. "We patched the blanket. It's not too bad. It's what our Lord taught us to do – to forgive."

These had to be two of the nicest people I had ever met, I decided. Let me set the scene for you. A simple stone house, rough wooden table and chairs, animals through an archway down a step. A bit of basic furniture, nativity-type clothing, an oil lamp on the table with the three of us sitting round it, friendly, the temperature was perfect – not as hot as it had been earlier. The room was a bit smelly in a farm kind of way, but so ... what's the word I want? Homely. Uncomplicated. With decent people in it. Just what a home should be like, I thought. You could have said they were poor, but really they were the richest people I had ever met.

And as I sat there looking round, thinking how wonderful it was here, Anna cut through my thoughts. "We always have a choice. Choosing to forgive sets us free."

"But what if people don't deserve it?" I sighed. "It's so unfair!"

"Surely you'll have seen that forgiveness is better than revenge?" Seth said with a chuckle. "Look what happened when you tried!"

I thought how miserable it was going to be with Trinity from now on, and I had to agree. Anna must have seen my dejected face. "Leave your troubles with the Lord Jesus," she said gently. "He will never let you down." I tried to smile, but didn't answer.

Seth gave me a punch across the table. "Hey, cheer up!" he said. "You can choose to forgive, just like we did!" And it came to me that we can choose to do right or wrong, and we can choose to forgive or not. Everyone has a choice. These people were doing what was right. Trinity chose to do what was wrong. It was her choice, and I might never be able to stop her. But I still had to choose to do the right thing myself, like the man in the olive grove had said.

Just as I was hoping Seth and Anna would let me sleep there for at least one night, if not for ever, there was a commotion outside. Anna was just saying that God made the world beautiful, but we spoil it with our selfish, evil behaviour, when Trinity came in. I felt that was kind of appropriate. Selfish, evil behaviour personified. Just at that moment I baulked at having to forgive her. She did look ugly, I thought. The only appealing thing about seeing her was that she had some kind of animal muck smeared all over her favourite pink trousers.

How could I possibly forgive her for ruining my life, I wondered, as she stamped her foot and demanded that we go. She was fed up of this stinking place, she said. She curled her lip up at Seth and Anna, and looked down her nose at them in her superior way.

She was so wrong about being better than them, I thought, trying not to grind my teeth at her lack of respect for my new friends. They offered her a drink but she sniffed haughtily and said, "What here, in this grimy hovel? You've got to be kidding." Then added to me, "Hurry up, moron, I'll wait outside," as she turned and left.

Seth put his arm round my shoulders as we walked towards the door. I was still hoping that he would ask me to stay, or hold her back for me while I ran away and hid, but he didn't. "I'll pray for you," he promised.

Anna gave me a hug. "Remember the sparrows," she whispered. "Remember that God cares about you, too."

"And remember to be merciful and forgive," said Seth. I didn't reply – I wasn't sure I could promise that. What was my life going to be like now?

sixteen

The Good Samaritan

On the way home, Trinity tried to push me off the carpet. Trying to get her own back, no doubt, or attempting to. No chance. I sat in the middle, cross-legged, and held my ground. I don't know why, really. At that point I wouldn't have minded falling into oblivion, if it meant I didn't have to live with her any more. But I couldn't let her have her own way. Of course I was much stronger than she was now, so she didn't stand a chance, not like when we were children.

Having said that, her strength might not be in her muscles, but it was certainly still in her tongue. With that vicious instrument she could make any sane person wither to nothing. She used it to good effect on the way home, but I'll leave that to your imagination.

Spencer's face was a picture when I told him about me pushing her off the carpet. He patted me on the back like I was a hero, and promised that soon we'd think of something else, as we hadn't managed to get rid of her permanently, yet. I wasn't sure. I was still mulling over the "be merciful and forgive" problem. I couldn't really explain all that to Spencer, because we were eating our sandwiches in the school canteen. Not the place for a sensible discussion.

If it were possible, The Worst Sister in the World was even worse to me than ever for the next few days, but that, I told myself gloomily, was my fault for pushing her off the carpet. Now I could hardly eat or drink without it being spiked with something – vinegar, chilli powder, sugar (on chips), salt (on cereal) ... I can't remember all the details now, but I do remember feeling almost permanently sick and/ or hungry.

I lived off packets of biscuits I bought from the corner shop on the way home from school. Revenge had backfired, but forgiving had to be impossible, too, I decided, after she deleted my geography course work. She just didn't deserve to be forgiven. But Seth had promised to pray, and the old man had, too, and I didn't want to let them down, so I tried my hardest for a while.

It didn't last long. I gave up after she put itching powder in my bed. That was a bad night. Mum was furious. She and Trinity shouted at each other while I had a shower then changed the sheets, then Winnie from next door banged on the wall and yelled to us to shut up and Mum and Trinity yelled back – it was pandemonium.

It was days before I got rid of the itching completely, and my skin was raw in places from the scratching.

By the time I managed to talk to Spencer properly, there was another adventure to tell him about. Trinity jumped out at me from behind the kitchen door one evening, shot lemon juice in my face from a squeezy plastic lemon, then while I was writhing and splashing my eyes with water at the sink (fortunately my glasses stopped the worst of it), she put the carpet behind me, shoved me hard, and off we flew.

I was still rubbing my eyes when we landed in ancient Rome, in a meeting of Christians in the home of a man called Nathaniel, still way back in time, although I wouldn't like to say exactly when. All I can tell you for sure was that it was some time after Jesus went back to heaven, and the people were wearing robes and togas.

We just arrived there, and nobody seemed to think anything of it, even though I must have looked really weird, wiping my sore eyes (has your sister ever thrown lemon juice in your face? Thought not. You don't know how lucky you are).

So there we were, me and Trinity, sitting on the carpet in this large, airy room, with about twenty or thirty other people, all adults of different ages. And from all walks of life by the look of it. Most people were sitting on wooden benches, though some were on the floor on brightly coloured cushions.

Everyone was listening respectfully to a man with a scroll, who was standing at the front. He was reading the story of the Good Samaritan. It's in the Bible – you might have heard it. It's a story Jesus told his followers, and they wrote it down so we could learn from it, too. It goes like this: a Jew gets beaten up and robbed on a remote road, then left for dead. Two religious people pass by on the other side, but a good Samaritan stops to help the man, cleans his wounds and takes him to an inn to be taken care of.

When the man had finished reading, there was a reverent pause while he rolled up the scroll, then he lifted his head and his hands up to heaven and started praying. Trinity snorted with derision, got up and walked out, but I stayed. Never in my life have I heard anyone pray like that man did. His prayer was honest, and powerful, and open, and you could tell that he meant every word. I can't remember what he said, but the thing that really struck me was how much it seemed like he was talking to a real person; a powerful but invisible friend.

Then the man began to talk, while the rest of us listened. His talking was powerful, too. He was a big man with dark skin and dark hair, like most of the people

I had met on the carpet journeys, and he had a bushy beard, which he stroked sometimes while he talked.

He really got into explaining the story; he made it like we were there. Man, I could almost feel the heat of the desert road. My heart was beating as the robbers got into place behind a rock, waiting for a passer-by to rob. I could almost feel the danger, hear the groaning of the man who had been robbed and smell the fear of the men who walked past the bleeding man in their fancy robes. I almost held my breath at the kindness of the Samaritan (Samaritans were enemies of the Jews in those days, apparently), as he risked helping the victim. I nearly cried when the man with the beard talked about doing good to your enemies; I almost knew that he was going to say that. There it was again – mercy. Surely, I was thinking, soon the carpet would be merciful to me?

Then, with tears in his eyes, the man talked about Jesus dying on the cross in our place. He was like the Good Samaritan, he said, who hadn't left the helpless robbed man to die. I tell you, this story was the best I'd ever heard. I was desperate to know more, but after another prayer, the meeting was over.

The people all got up and started chatting to each other. I wasn't sure what to do, but the man who had been speaking came over to me. "Welcome, brother," he said with a warm smile. "Peace be with you."

"Thank you," I said, my heart still full of the story and its meaning. Then I added, "And also with you," because I heard someone say it to someone else behind me.

"Have you been in Rome long?" he asked.

Rome, I thought, that's different, but just shook my head. "Just arrived."

The people in the room drifted off, one by one, while I was saying to the man that I loved the way he told the story. His name was Michael, and he was another one of those warm and friendly people that I knew the carpet wanted me to meet (I was kind of getting used to it by that time!). He was saying how wonderful the Scriptures are, and that's when it dawned on me that the story he had told was from the Bible. Well it was all dropping into place into my mind, while he was saying a bit more about the story, and I was saying that I had borrowed a copy of the Bible and had started reading it, when Nathaniel's wife came and said to us both, "But you must stay and eat with us," and Michael agreed we must, so that was that.

I suppose she thought we were together or something; anyway I didn't object. I felt drawn to these people, in just the same way as I had in some of the other places the carpet had taken us to. I didn't know where Trinity had disappeared to, but I didn't care. The less I saw of her the better.

We were treated to an amazing meal with about twenty courses, just the four of us, served by helpful servants. It was a pleasant change to be able to eat without testing everything first, to see if Trinity had spiked it with anything. One of the courses we had early on was goat stew. Michael said, "Lovely goat," that's how I know. It's OK you know, goat, done properly, but some of the other meat looked a bit weird, so I decided not to ask what it was, and just ate it and concentrated on remembering the room, so I could paint it later.

During the meal we (I say we, but it was mostly them) started off talking about the Good Samaritan story and what Michael had said about it, then the three of them (sorry, I can't remember what Nathaniel's wife's name was) talked about danger and their enemies, and how they could keep themselves hidden and yet still meet together.

It was obviously a bit of a hot topic, but I didn't really understand it at the time. I wished afterwards I'd paid more attention, but it was so weird being there, and the food was weird, and I was too busy looking at the mosaics and the vases and archways and stuff, trying not to spill anything down me. I'm not used to eating while half-lying on my side on a settee with cushions. It was embarrassing how much dripped down my face and clothes.

We had already had several courses when Nathaniel turned to me. "So, what does your family do, Paul?"

I thought quickly. How could I explain that my dad had a job in insurance and my mum worked in an office? "Um, my dad's not around any more," I said in the end. "It's just my mum and my sister and me."

"Sorry to hear that," Michael said, and Nathaniel and his wife nodded in sympathy.

"So, how long have you been a Christian?" asked Michael. They were obviously wanting to include me in the conversation.

Another difficult question! "I'm not really sure what being a Christian means," I replied. "I've never been to a meeting like this before."

"Oh! So, what brought you today?"

Well I could hardly say the carpet, could I? So I told them that I had borrowed a Bible and had begun to pray. Michael nodded and smiled. "How much do you know about being a Christian?"

"Not much," I admitted. "But I'd like to know," I added. I did want to know, I really did.

Michael smiled at me. "You need to repent and believe," he said, leaning across the table.

I must have looked a bit blank.

"Do you want me to go over that with you?"

"Yes please."

"OK, well you have to confess your sins to God.

You have to turn from your old ways and follow Jesus' way instead. It's like getting on a different path. That's repentance."

I nodded again. "I see." I didn't see terribly well, but it sounded like what the prophet had said about turning from your wicked ways, which was encouraging.

"Believing is closely tied to repentance," Michael continued. "Without faith you can not please God. You have to believe that Jesus is the Messiah, the Son of God, who took the punishment we deserved by dying for us on the cross. Do you believe that?"

I pursed my lips and thought for a moment. "So Jesus really did die on a cross?"

"Yes, he did. For you and for me, and for every one of us. He who knew no sin became sin for us. The punishment we deserved, he took on himself so that we could go free." And at that moment, I knew he did. I thought of Anna and Seth and all that they had told me about Jesus.

"I do believe that," I told him.

Michael leaned over towards me over the table and looked into my eyes. "But it's no good believing if you are going to turn back. There is a price to pay."

I was puzzled. "What do you mean?"

He looked at me with something in his eyes I could hardly grasp. It was a sincerity and earnestness, and a determination and a fierceness rolled into one. "Well bless you, you have no idea, do you?"

"Idea about what?" I asked tucking into something on a bone that had once been alive. The food was good, but I was starting to feel uncomfortable.

"Persecution, hardship, prison ... if you are a follower of Christ Jesus, you will be persecuted, maybe killed." Well I have to say, that didn't sound so appealing and my face must have shown it. Michael shook his head sadly and looked away.

"Why?" I asked. It was all so confusing. "Aren't Christians good people? Why should that happen?"

"There is a battle in spiritual places," Nathaniel told me. "Satan doesn't want the kingdom of God to grow, so he does what he can to stamp us out. Because if you are a Christian you are in God's kingdom. It's a whole body of people, spreading to every tribe and nation – people who worship God in spirit and in truth."

"I've got a lot to learn," I admitted. "I did visit a prophet in prison, once, though," I remembered. "He was a believer in God. And he talked about people needing to turn from their wicked ways."

"Well then you know what it's like," Michael said with a cry. "They track us down, throw us into prison, burn our homes, throw us to the lions ..."

I must have been staring, but he smiled at me with his burning, earnest gaze. "You don't have to fear, though, lad. They can kill our bodies, but they can't kill our souls! For true followers of Christ there will be treasures in heaven. It is a privilege to suffer for our Lord. We are walking in his footsteps. When they hurled their insults at him he did not retaliate. Even death couldn't hold him! The devil thought he had triumphed, but Jesus rose again from the dead, then ascended into heaven! And so will we, on the last day, if we stay faithful to the end."

I was just about to ask about rising again from the dead when there was a knock at the door and a servant came in. He didn't beat about the bush. "The girl who came with the visitor, she's in prison."

There was a deathly silence. A mean hope sprung up in me, though – Trinity in prison – that had to be good news!

seventeen

Wrong Person

I covered my mouth with a napkin, so the others couldn't see me trying not to smile at the thought of Trinity in a cell. As you might expect, the others reacted completely differently. All their faces fell and they stood up – Michael, Nathaniel and his wife. Even the servants looked grave.

"She's my sister," I told them, as they all looked at me. I expect they thought I would be devastated. I wasn't. Trinity in prison! I had to stop myself from punching the air and shouting "YES!" at the top of my voice. The carpet must be getting revenge for me at last!

Michael spoke as if this was the worst thing ever, as he strode for the door. "We must see if we can get her released."

"I wouldn't worry," I said, getting up and brushing some crumbs from my trousers. "I'm sure she'll be fine." They ignored me completely, and Nathaniel's wife let out a sob.

"But Michael, it's so dangerous. They know who you are." She was wringing her hands. "They will take you instead!"

"Yeah, honestly, don't worry, Michael," I said, joining the little group by the door and trying to look nonchalant. "My sister can take care of herself. Honestly."

Michael picked up his cloak and put his hand on my shoulder. "No, Paul, you don't understand."

You don't, I thought with an inner groan, seeing that he was intent on going to try and get her released, but I couldn't think of anything else to say. Michael turned to Nathaniel, who was already being handed his cloak by the servant. "Will you come with me, brother?" he asked.

"I will," he said. His wife clung to him for a minute, then fastened his cloak with a pin for him and kissed him, with tears in her eyes. "Take care, I will be praying," she promised, looking at the three of us, so with my heart sinking I supposed I'd have to go, too.

Nothing good would come of this, I thought, as we stepped out into the Roman street.

Walking down the road in ancient Rome is an experience, believe me. Massive buildings towered all round, some with huge pillars and arches – awesome. The noise and the smells weren't awesome, though, they were totally gross. Real chariots were going up and down the road, and horses, and donkeys and carts of all shapes and sizes. Hungry-looking dogs were wandering about scavenging whatever scraps they could find. People were milling about all over the place, yelling and selling stuff, and a chain of thin, ragged people went by in single file; I suppose they were slaves.

It was only a few minutes' walk to the prison, but it was an experience I will never forget – the whole scene was like a history book come alive. There was so much to see, I wanted to look around, but couldn't do that as much as I wanted, because I had a job to keep up, and not get lost in the throng of people. Michael and Nathaniel were talking to each other; I couldn't hear what they were saying exactly, but I gathered they were discussing what they would say at the prison.

After a few blocks, and me nearly getting run over by a cart, Michael turned into a dark side street with houses leaning over. Creepy hardly covers it. A cart of filthy straw stood in the street, and Michael and Nathaniel stopped by it. "This will do, wait here," Michael said to me, putting his arm round my shoulder. I was feeling bewildered.

"Don't you want me to come in with you?" I asked.

"It's too dangerous." He lifted back his shoulders as if taking on a big task. "But I'll do my best to free your sister." I looked at his face. It's difficult to explain;

in one way he looked desperate, but in another way it was like he was waiting to be transformed. "Give Phaedra my pottery and the parchments," he said to Nathaniel, his voice thick with emotion. "And my winter cloak to Benjamin."

"I'm not waiting here! I'm coming in with you!" Nathaniel remonstrated.

"No, brother, there's no need, and you have a wife to take care of."

Nathaniel grasped Michael's shoulders. "I'm not leaving you." The two of them seemed to have forgotten me. A feeling of dread was spreading from the pit of my stomach. I wanted to yell, "She's not worth it, just leave her here, she's getting the justice she deserves," but they were so caught up deciding who would go that when I tried to say something, they ignored me.

In the end, they both went, and I waited alone in that dingy side street by the cart. I have to tell you, it wasn't a nice wait. There were three reasons. Firstly, I didn't want Trinity to be freed. Secondly, I didn't want anything to happen to Michael or Nathaniel, and the way they had been talking, it sounded like they were taking on a big risk. Thirdly, several people passing by stared at me, and I don't think it was because I was wearing western clothes. They looked like they might be planning to rob me, or kill me, or grab me to sell me as a slave.

I ignored them and tried to look nonchalant and pretended to tie my shoelaces several times in the time I stood there. I don't know how long it was. I suspect it wasn't anything like as long as it felt.

At last Trinity came out with Nathaniel. She was brushing her clothes down; her face was like thunder. "How DARE they put me in that stinking, filthy prison, how DARE they!" she seethed. Her pony tail bobbed up and down and she looked just about as evil as she could be.

"Where's Michael?" I asked Nathaniel.

"They took him in her place," Nathaniel told me, almost in a whisper. I could see the grief on his face, like a dark, deep shadow.

"Why?" I asked, my breathing beginning to come in gasps.

"Your sister isn't a Christian, so they didn't want to keep her."

"Arrested me when I left this clown's house," Trinity told me loftily, pointing to Nathaniel viciously with her finger as if it was all his fault. "The biggest mistake they ever made, I'll tell you. I'll take them to court over this. How DARE they touch me!"

"Why did they take Michael instead?" I asked Nathaniel, trying to stop tears coming to my eyes, but it was Trinity who replied.

"I told them straight, when I saw him, 'Him, he's

the one who was reading from the scroll and praying. If it's Christians you want, you should get him, and let me go free." She curled her face up into a horrid sneer. "He admitted that I had only been in the meeting for a second, and that I wasn't one of them. So they let me go," she said. "At least they got the right person *that* time."

My heart was beating in my chest, my breath was coming in gasps, and I felt weak at the knees. I held on to the filthy cart for support. "What will they do to him?" I whispered to Nathaniel, who could barely speak.

"They will send him home, to be with his Lord," Nathaniel whispered.

"You mean kill him?"

Nathaniel nodded and tore his robe. I felt like tearing mine, but sweatshirts don't tear easily. "He took her place, just as Jesus took ours."

I felt like screaming and yelling, charging into the prison, throwing You Know Who in and getting Michael back, but I knew it would be useless. "We'd better go home," I said to Trinity through gritted teeth, "before you ruin everyone's life."

"No kidding, I don't want to stay in this filthy hell-hole."

Nathaniel took me to one side as we began the short, sad walk back to his house. "Michael forgave her, when they took him. You must forgive her, too.

Now Michael will take hold of the life that is truly life. Take courage, my friend. Michael prayed that God would forgive her, because she didn't know what she was doing. You must forgive her, too."

I ground my teeth in answer. I felt like pushing her under the wheels of a chariot.

eighteen

Last Trip

The last trip was short, and so awesome, it's difficult for me to describe.

On that particular day I was sitting on my bed doing some revision on the history of medicine when Trinity came in. The carpet was on the floor and she stood next to it, in the doorway, and leant on the door. I ignored her, wondering what she wanted, ready to defend anything she might want to "borrow", which meant steal, because she never gave anything back.

Anyway, she just stood there and I ignored her, so she went away. I was relieved; it made me tense, her standing there like that, not knowing what she was thinking or intending.

Then she came back and this time she stood on the edge of the carpet. "Want to come on?" she asked, in a reasonable tone.

"Why?" I was suspicious, of course.

She shrugged. "I'm bored."

I hesitated, thinking back to the horrors of the last trip and what Michael had had to do to save her. "Is that why you chucked lemon juice in my face last time?" I asked. "Were you bored?"

"Well, there was no point just asking, you'd have said no."

Too right I would have, I thought. "So what makes you think I'll say yes this time? A good man died because of you in Rome."

She curled her lip. "He didn't *have* to save me, he chose to. Leave me there next time, if you like."

I said nothing, but gritted my teeth. If I'd have had my way, I'd have left her every time, I thought. I went back to my homework. Some of the treatments I tried not to imagine her having with glee, like getting her leg sawn off without anaesthetic, or having a hole drilled into her skull to stop a headache.

Anyway, she went out of the door and I wasn't quite so relieved this time, with good reason, because she came back with an enormous pair of scissors. More like shears they were, than scissors.

"Get on the rug or I'll cut it up," she said, brandishing the scissors in a dangerous fashion.

"Why are you so desperate to go somewhere?" I asked, panicking a bit, playing for time. She had been through spates of cutting up my favourite things before.

"Because I hate my life here and want to make a new start somewhere else."

Wow, I thought, she doesn't intend to come back. "But if you make a new start somewhere else, I won't be able to get back." That was lame. My welfare wasn't high on her list of priorities.

"Then you'll have to make a new life, too, won't you," she said with a "why should I care" kind of a shrug. "I'll try not to go somewhere where you'll get put in prison," she added, with a strange gleam in her eye that I didn't like. Did I trust her? Not one bit.

I thought quickly. She seemed totally serious. She snapped the scissors open and closed a few times, for effect, and stared at me defiantly. Massive scissors they were, I don't know where she got them. Maybe she bought them specially.

"What if you don't like it where we go," I asked, trying to sound nonchalant, but keeping my eye on the scissors and saving my revision file, just in case.

"We'll keep going places until I find one I like." I nodded. That explained Rome. And it wasn't good. Because if she liked a place, I would probably hate it. I was really beginning to panic now, watching her snap the scissors open and closed. "Why don't you go with Juliette or some other of your friends?"

"You know it only works for us two."

I did. I was stalling and she knew it. "What if I don't want to?"

"I'll cut up the rug."

"Then you'll never be able to go anywhere."

"So it'll be the same as if you never go with me then, won't it?" As she was speaking, she got down on her knees on the carpet and started cutting off the corner furthest away, with her back to me.

"Stop that!" I yelled in alarm, hoping she was bluffing, but I could hear the sound of cutting fibres. She turned round, and with a mean smile, held up the corner of the carpet in her hand to show me, then flapped it. Annoyed isn't the word for it. I was furious. Livid. All the angry words you can think of, put together, mashed up and spat out. I couldn't think any longer, I hurled myself on to her to stop her and of course, off we flew.

Somehow the scissors had managed to fly off the carpet, but not before You Know Who had slashed my hand with them – I was trying to stop the bleeding as Trinity suddenly stopped and screamed at something she had seen behind me. We were not alone on the carpet. I turned round, and I think I must have just sat there with my mouth wide open for a few seconds, bleeding hand forgotten.

Our visitor was a very tall man, like the basketball players you see on sports programmes, but not black or white, more Middle Eastern, standing silently on the far edge of our carpet, watching us. He was wearing shining white robes, a bit Greek style, with a golden belt, and he was holding a sword in his hands. It was truly awesome – like being in the middle of a fantasy film. Trinity fainted. I suppose I should have put her in the recovery position, but it didn't occur to me at the time.

Behind and below the man, I could see that we were in space, far, far above the world. It was the first time I had ever seen anything below the carpet. I heard myself gasp as I looked below to our planet, looking like a fragile blue patterned marble, suspended in space. It was truly awesome, totally breathtaking.

Then, as if that wasn't enough of a shock, the carpet began to turn and a dragon appeared in the sky – an enormous red dragon, flinging stars down to the earth with a ferocity to match Trinity in a foul mood. Only a lot more powerful, you understand. It was incredibly frightening, in a fear-of-the-dark horror movie kind of way.

My eyes must have been nearly popping out of my head and I was really glad that we didn't get too near the dragon – I was just beginning to panic that he would notice us when we turned in another direction. At first I was relieved, but only for a second. I couldn't see what we were heading towards, because we were heading towards a light. As we got closer and closer to the light it got brighter – it got so bright that I began to feel truly terrified, like I had never been scared in my life before. I mean, not ever. Nothing comes close. Nothing. Ever. Not even that dragon.

nineteen

The Conclusion

Blinding light filled the atmosphere, like air fills a room. It was shining from somewhere high above us, so bright I had to shield my eyes as we got closer, and the noise of it was like a hurricane or waves crashing.

And there was a presence there that was so powerful that I thought I was going to die, just being there. I felt filthy. I curled into a ball on the carpet, shielding my head with my arms. At that moment nothing else mattered, nothing; there was nothing but the terror of the light. I even forgot that the shining man was there (I think he might have been an angel), and that I was on a flying carpet. Then gradually the noise and the light passed and I sat up again a bit, panting and shocked. And then I had a glimpse, the smallest, less than a millisecond glimpse of the most beautiful, awesome place where the colours were bright and everyone was filled with unspeakable happiness, and then it was gone.

I turned to look at Trinity, but she was still out of it.

"She chose not to see," said the man in white. Now I was shocked again, to hear his voice. "She will be given another chance."

I nodded, but I couldn't speak. My heart was still pounding like I don't know what, my palms were sweating, my breath was coming in gasps, like I'd just run a marathon.

The man sort of smiled. He seemed friendly, which was a relief, and not frightening exactly, just awesome, especially with that sword. "What are you thinking?" he asked.

I still wasn't feeling quite myself after that experience. I tried to speak, and opened my mouth, but only a squeak came out. The man/angel reached out and touched my shoulder with his sword, which strangely made me feel a bit stronger. "Speak," he said, and I gulped and found my tongue.

"I have never seen anything like any of this before. Nothing even comes close."

"You have seen part of a mystery." I nodded, still too overcome to talk. "Were you frightened of the dragon?" he continued.

I thought about it. "Yes," I managed eventually, as my heart rate and breathing returned to normal. "But not anything like as scared as I was of the place with the light. And that beautiful place, what was that?"

"The dragon is a picture of God's enemy, who deceives the whole world. The light you saw was the light of Jesus Christ, and the beautiful place is the paradise of God."

"That dragon, who was sweeping stars out of the sky and chucking them down onto our world, he's God's enemy?" I asked in astonishment, and the man nodded.

"In time, all living beings will fall down to worship the true God. But for now the dragon has some power on earth."

"I see," I said. The man gave me a bit of time to think about it, which was useful. It was dawning on me that there was something much bigger going on than I had imagined. Bigger than people, bigger than politics and wars and horrid sisters. "So if that's a picture, is there a real God, and a real enemy, and a real paradise of God?"

"Yes."

"Are the troubles on earth part of the thing with the dragon?"

"Yes."

"Is he making trouble?"

"Yes."

I was confused. "But if there's nothing we can do about it ..."

"Everyone has a choice. God has made the way."

I nodded, still a bit overawed by the whole light thing. I was trying to remember where I had heard that thing about choice before. The man in the olive grove! And Seth and Anna, of course! And the Good Samaritan ...

The man cut across my thoughts. "Would you like me to tell you about the reason for your journeys?"

"Yes please, but can you give me a minute? I'm feeling a bit overwhelmed."

The man nodded again. It's difficult to find the right words to describe those few moments, but if you could have taken a screen shot right then, there was me in the middle of the carpet, Trinity behind me, flat out, the man in front of me. I was sitting, he was standing, and he was tall, dressed in white and holding a shining sword. I had to crane my neck to look up at him. The carpet was missing the corner that You Know Who had hacked off, but it was still flying fine – gliding I should say, through space, with the world far below us.

After a few minutes, the man touched me with his sword again, which gave me more strength, then laid it down to the side and sat down opposite me. That was good; I didn't have to crane my neck so much.

"All the people you met, all the places you have been to, were all to show you God's free gift of mercy. You can take hold of this grace."

I pursed my lips and thought. All this was to show me that I needed mercy?

"You are thinking that it's your sister who needs mercy and forgiveness, not you?"

I nodded. "She is beyond what you can imagine, believe me."

"What about you, do you need mercy?" That was a good question. I thought about it, as the carpet continued to glide gently through space. I thought about how filthy I had felt in the presence of the light and I was confused.

"It's her, she's the bad one," I managed eventually.

"And you? Do you need forgiveness too?"

I thought again and I knew I did. I thought about wanting her dead, enjoying the thought of her suffering. "Well, I'm not perfect," I admitted. "Still, she ..." and I stopped.

"Everyone falls short of God's glory. In him is light, and there is no darkness at all."

I nodded. I think I saw that. "So I need forgiveness, too?"

"Yes."

"Wasn't all this to show me how to get revenge on my sister?" Even as I said it, the truth was dawning on me, but it was the man who put it into a word.

"No."

I sat there, taking this in, while the world turned

slowly below. The whole carpet thing wasn't about her, it was about me! "And I have to forgive my enemies?"

"Yes. All who have been forgiven and who forgive, will rise and live again."

"Does that mean go to the paradise of God? To that beautiful place?"

"Yes. Jesus is preparing a place for each one. All who wash their robes will have the right to go through the gates into the city. All this will be done on the last day."

I thought about it. The whole scope of the matter was blowing my mind, although in a way it was so simple. But there was one thing that didn't seem right, and it bothered me. People don't get what they deserve in our world. Like me. And like the prophet – thrown into prison for telling the truth and trying to help.

As I was thinking of the words to express the way I felt, the man said, "God is just and merciful. All who have been faithful will receive their reward at the end of time."

That made me smile. "Justice," I said. "Will it be the same for everyone?"

The man didn't actually smile like we do, but there was a kind of joy emanating from him. "Yes."

"And the gardener and the master of the manor and those girls?"

"Mercy and grace are for all those who have chosen to walk in God's ways during their lives on earth. Judgment will come to those who refuse."

I nodded, and looked at my hand, which had stopped bleeding by then.

The man looked at my hand, too. He knew what I was thinking. "You must leave judgment to God," he told me.

"I'm told that God cares for me," I told him, thinking of Seth and Anna.

"God loved the world so much, he sent his only Son so that whoever believes in him will not die, but have eternal life."

"Jesus took my place," I said quietly, remembering what Michael had said, and even as I said it, something beautiful filled my soul. Something good, something precious. And as I sat on the carpet, there with the angel, I cried until I had no more tears, then I laughed until I couldn't laugh any more, and then I was filled with a peace that I can't describe to you.

"It is by grace you are saved, through faith," said the angel, when I was at last still. "Never doubt that. Worship God and walk in his ways, as many have done before, and many still do." I nodded, thinking of all the people I had met. Elishah and Bildad, the prophet, Seth and Anna, the gardener, the man in the olive grove, Nathaniel and his wife, and Michael.

"What about Michael?" I remembered.

"All who believe will be received into the eternal paradise of God, when their life on earth is done."

I thought again of that tiny glimpse of that most wonderful place and was glad. I didn't think I would ever see things the same way after seeing that. "Thank you for talking to me," I said to the angel, as we landed back in my room. Trinity stirred and the man stood up – I couldn't believe it, his head nearly reached the ceiling!

"I am only doing my duty. God sent me to you to show you the way."

I stood up too, with the man towering above me. "I appreciate that, thank you," I said, looking up. "I don't know how I'm going to be merciful to Trinity, but I will try. I thought the carpet was going to help me get revenge, though."

"God will judge justly on the last day. Revenge is not for you to take. His Spirit is with you. He will give you the strength to persevere in times of trial."

I nodded, thinking of the prophet, and the gardener. "Would you like a cup of tea before you go?" I asked the man, as there was a slight pause in the conversation, hoping as I said it that Mum wasn't downstairs with Laurence.

He didn't answer, he just said, "May the grace of God remain with you always," then he was gone. I stood there for a few minutes, hardly able to take in what had happened. Trinity woke up, while I was still standing there in a daze. She rubbed her eyes and yawned.

"What am I doing on your floor?" she asked in horror, as much to herself as to me, when she discovered where she was. Brushing down her clothes, she walked quickly out.

It was then that I realised that the carpet had gone – the man must have taken it with him. But I didn't need it any more. I started to get out my art materials. I had a lot to paint.

Revenge of the Flying Carpet

Reading Group Questions

1. Paul and Trinity are twins, but there are many ways they are not alike. What would you say are the main differences between them?

2. Paul meets several people on his journeys. (The soldiers, the King, the old man in the olive grove, the prophet, the gardener, Seth and Anna, and Michael.) Who would you most like to have met, if it were you on the flying carpet? Why?

3. Do you think Spencer is a good friend? Paul feels the man in the olive grove understands how he feels. Do you have someone you feel understands you? When people talk to you, do you try to understand how they are feeling?

4. Why do you think Paul experienced a sense of freedom when he returned to the place where he had been imprisoned in the dungeon, to find it in ruins?

5. Paul finds it helpful to paint his experiences. He also found it helpful to pray. How do you like to express yourself? Do you pray, the way Paul does? Do you think you would find it helpful if you did?

6. Why was the prophet in prison? Was he a criminal? Are there people who are imprisoned for their faith in God today?

7. What do these words mean: righteousness, justice, mercy, grace, revenge, forgiveness? Name some of the reasons Paul wants to get revenge on Trinity. Can you understand that feeling? Is there anyone you would like to get revenge on, who has hurt you in some way?

8. Why does Paul describe Seth and Anna as being "rich people" when they have so few material possessions? How rich do you think are you?

9. What do you think is better – revenge or forgiveness? Why? Can you imagine being able to forgive people who have hurt you? Seth and Anna forgave the man who allowed his goats to eat their blanket. Michael forgave Trinity for betraying him. Why did they decide to forgive? Do you think it would have been a hard thing to do?

10. What was different about the last trip? Was Paul more afraid of the dragon or the light? Why? What did Paul discover about the reason for his trips on the flying carpet? Does he get revenge in the end? Does he get justice? Do you think the book could have ended in a different way?

You can find more questions on the Dernier Publishing website.

Would you like to read more books like this one? You can find these, and more, on the Dernier Publishing website: **www.dernierpublishing.com**

More books from Dernier Publishing:

London's Gone
By J. M. Evans

London has been bombed by terrorists. The government has been wiped out, there is widespread power failure and throughout England riots have begun.

Maria saw the war planes fly over her home near London and watched in horror as the smoke rose from the direction of the city. Now she must make a hazardous journey to safety with her sister and a Christian friend.

For Maria, the journey is also inside herself, as she is forced to face issues that she has never had to consider before and begins to discover a side to life that she never knew existed.

"I just couldn't put this book down." — **Gilly**

"Really well written." — **Laura**

"Very exciting, full of atmosphere." — **Eleanor**

The Only Way

By Gareth Rowe

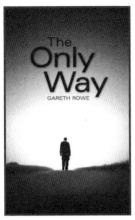

When a miserable, disaffected teenager meets the beautiful and mysterious Lily, he discovers a new way to live, the only way. Later, when Lily's life in danger, he is willing to risk everything to save her, but time and circumstances are against him. How can he live, if she doesn't survive?

A story of hope for young people.

"The Only Way *is a moving, fast-paced, gripping and genius piece of writing. A must read for everyone."*
    — G.P. Taylor, New York Times bestselling author

"The Only Way *hooked me straight away ... Brilliant and funny writing."* **— Jackie Kay MBE**

"*This is a very good book with some exciting moments."* **— George**

"*I enjoyed this book and it was an interesting read because the author made really exciting things happen."* **— Naomi**

What is a Christian?

If you have read this book, and wondered what it means to be a Christian, here's a quick explanation:

First we need to go back to the beginning.

Christians believe that God made the heavens and the earth, and everything in it. At first everything was perfect, but sadly, people deliberately disobeyed God, and "sin" came into the world. That's bad things like lying, stealing and cheating. We have all done these things, and had these things done to us. We know what it's like.

Our sin separates us from God (who is perfect in every way), so we needed someone to take the punishment in our place. Justice has to be done. Sin has to be paid for.

Because he loved us so much and wanted to make a way for us to live with him again, God the Father sent his Son, Jesus, into the world. Jesus was born in Bethlehem at the time of the Romans, and lived a perfect life. Jesus took on himself the punishment we deserved for our sin, when he died on a cross – he hadn't sinned like we do, but he died in our place. (It's a bit like someone paying someone else's debt.) Three days later, Jesus rose from the dead – he defeated death!

We don't deserve God's forgiveness, but if we are truly

sorry for our sin and decide to walk in his ways instead of ours, he not only promises to forgive us, but gives us his Holy Spirit to live with us forever. So when we are a Christian, we will go on living with God in heaven after our bodies die.

So a Christian is someone who:

- has turned to God
- has had their sins forgiven
- follows Jesus (that means following his example)
- has the Holy Spirit living in them
- is looking forward to heaven!

We know all this though the Bible, which is God's word – it's a great book. :-)

Would you like to be a Christian?

If you would like to become a Christian you need to take the following steps:

1. Be sure it's what you want to do. Think carefully. Are you truly sorry for your sin? Do you really want to follow Jesus?

2. If you do, you need to pray. That means talk to God. You can do it anywhere, any time. (Not only

did he make the whole world and everything in it, but God knows everything about us and hears us when we pray. Awesome!)

3. Here's a first prayer you can use if you like. (It starts Dear Lord – many prayers say "Lord" when they are talking about God, because when you are a Christian, Jesus becomes the Lord of your life, which means you do what he wants, not what you want … you will find out more about this as you grow as a Christian.)

Dear Lord,

I'm truly sorry for my sin. I realise now that my sin has stopped me from knowing you in the past, but I believe you died in my place. I'd like to follow you from now on. Please forgive me and send me your Holy Spirit, so I will be with you forever.

Amen

(Amen is a word often used at the end of a prayer. It means "let it be so".)

Now you need to get to know God!

Here are some steps you need to take:

- First, tell someone you have prayed. Who will

you tell? Do it right now! You can contact us, too – we would love to hear from you.

- Read the Bible. Find the book of Matthew (it's the first book of the New Testament), get yourself a bookmark, and start reading! Read a bit every day. You can read the Bible online if you haven't got a Bible yourself.

- Carry on praying. You can pray all the time, any time, anywhere – it is the most wonderful, amazing thing to talk to God who made the whole world and everything in it! You might like to just talk about how you feel. You might like to thank him for the good things in your life. You might like to ask him to help you with things you find difficult. It's fine to make up your own prayer – you can just talk, as if you were talking to a close friend or a loving father, because from now on Jesus will be your friend and God will be your Father in heaven! Or you can find some prayers online or in a book if you like. You can pray out loud or in your head because God even knows the thoughts of our hearts.

- Go to church with a friend or your family. Everyone who is a Christian needs to spend time with other Christians. If you don't know any other Christians, pray the Lord will help you find some, especially if you live in a country where there aren't many Christians and churches.

Remember this:

- *God loves you more than you can imagine!*

- *He knows everything about you, even your thoughts.*

- *He will always be with you – he will never abandon you or leave you alone.*

- *If God's Holy Spirit lives in you, you have been "born again" in your spirit.*

- *If you have asked for forgiveness and are truly sorry, you will be forgiven – it's a promise!*

- *Because we are human, we will keep on getting it wrong, but every time we ask for forgiveness, we will be washed clean once again.*

However you feel, trust in God. You know how on a cloudy day you can't see the sun? It's still there, though! In the same way, you might not always *feel* that God is with you, but he *is there* just the same.

If you have any questions, or would you like to contact any of our authors, please do so through the contact form on the Dernier Publishing website:

www.dernierpublishing.com/contact